MISCHIEF NIGHT

JAMES KAINE

Cover design by: Damonza

Edited by: Heather Ann Larson

For my Mom.

Thanks for watching Halloween with me all those years ago!

AUTHOR'S NOTE

A few times in this book, you will see the word Samhain.

Contrary to popular belief, it is not pronounced SAM-HANE. The proper pronunciation is **SOW-IN**.

Do with that information what you will.

CHAPTER 1

October 30, 1979

Rain splashed Jack Kelly's face as he walked through the doors of the sanitarium. Vowing to never return, he dropped to his knees, arms outstretched as he drank in his newfound freedom. He praised Ba'al's surrogate for granting it. The muddy ground stained the white hospital gown. The sparse garment did little to protect him from the late autumn chill.

But Jack didn't care. He was free.

He had been writing his latest sermon in his room. The tremors from the evening's shock therapy wracked his body, making it difficult to hold a pen. He wasn't allowed to have pens or pencils, as they could be used as weapons. Fortunately, Mick, the idiot orderly, provided an easy target for pick-pocketing. Over the past few hours, Jack filled an entire roll of toilet paper with writings.

As he started on a new paragraph, a loud crash from

behind startled him. Turning toward the commotion, his eyes locked on to the shape at his door. It was the hulking figure of Wallace Little, another inmate at the illustrious institution.

Jack was surprised. Wallace had been incarcerated at Pine Hill for as long as he could remember. At six foot three and built like a brick shithouse, Wallace was an impressive specimen, but Jack never heard him speak. He kept to himself, doing puzzles or reading the limited selection of books and magazines scattered around the rec room, keeping his bald head down more often than not. But at that moment, looking into his onyx eyes, Jack understood he was a dark angel—an angel sent by Ba'al. The reason he was sent tonight would remain to be seen.

His liberator didn't linger. He moved down the hall, the sound of splintering wood accompanying his departure. Jack seized the opportunity and followed.

He had little time to celebrate his newfound freedom. He rose and approached the small security booth by the gate. Inside was a guard, a stout man in his sixties. He looked to be sleeping, but his broken neck and dead eyes staring at the booth's ceiling told a different story. A displaced vertebra stretched the skin from the inside, threatening to rip through the flesh. His lifeless eyes registered the shock and horror of his final moments.

Jack searched the corpse. The deceased possessed a baton and a can of pepper spray but no firearm. Those would suffice.

Weapons were procured, but his hospital attire

would present a problem in the elements. The deceased offered a solution. Jack worked fast to swap garments. As soon as he was done, he exited the booth and made a run for the tree line and out of the view of the searchlights.

The sound of the commotion surrounding the breakout faded as Jack fled deeper into the woods. He didn't know the area well; he had lived in another part of the state before his capture. The asylum was a good distance from where he had led his congregation. It didn't matter. Ba'al would guide him.

In a small clearing, Jack rested beneath a large white oak. The tree provided scant protection from the rain, drops continuing to pelt his face. He didn't mind. He was free to continue Ba'al's work, a mission his incarceration had prevented for half a decade.

Jack remembered the first time he met Ba'al. He was living on the streets of Chicago. Seven months had passed since his return from Vietnam, and he found himself in a country that had abandoned him. Protestors at the airport spat on him, calling him *baby killer*. He fought for his country and came back empty-handed, lacking even the respect of his fellow citizens.

The only thing he did bring back was a predilection toward opiates. His addiction would render him homeless mere months after his return.

Jack journeyed from shelter to shelter, concerned with little else than finding his next fix. He didn't care about survival. He had no family and carried out horrid acts in the name of combating communism. Jack never considered killing himself, but he wasn't afraid of death. He would welcome it.

Death arrived on a rainy night in 1971, but not to take him. It came to recruit him. The sharp-dressed man approached him in an alley and introduced himself as Bill. The man treated Jack to a hot meal at a diner, his first in weeks. As they spoke, Jack understood him to be Ba'al, one of the chief demons of hell. The man promised him salvation if he could deliver an army.

After dinner, Ba'al brought Jack to a secluded cabin deep in the woods. Over the next three days, he detoxed. Sweat soaked his shaking body while the toxins exited, his sight filled with hallucinations of demons, hellfire, and blood. In the vision, he saw Ba'al's true form and pledged eternal allegiance to his demon master.

On the fourth morning, Jack awoke in a puddle of drool and piss. Ba'al was gone, leaving no evidence he was ever there. For a moment, Jack questioned his recollection, but he believed it was real. More than that, he had a purpose.

Over the next year, he traversed the state, looking to recruit wayward souls with the promise they could have everything they desired. Jack brought them to the cabin, where he would spend three days inflicting pain and torture, mirroring the seventy-two hours of suffering he had experienced. Some died, but Jack didn't mourn them. If they wouldn't become Ba'al's subjects, they would be sacrificed in his honor. Either way, Jack's dark lord would be satisfied.

In 1973, the cops found him. A firefight at the cabin claimed the lives of his five disciples. Jack was wounded but survived. The judge found him unfit to stand trial and remanded him to Pine Hill.

Continuing his ministry inside proved frustrating. His fellow inmates were too psychologically disturbed to reach. Among them, one appeared to understand the gospel, yet he was a demented sexual predator, unfit to be a true follower.

His thoughts snapped Jack back to the present and made him wonder. *Did Oliver make it out as well*?

Despite his shortcomings, Oliver had his uses. His enthusiasm, manipulated with the right incentive, was evident. A voice, summoned by his thoughts, spoke from behind.

"Father!"

Turning, he saw Oliver Craft running toward him. The man was short, with a wispy frame and stringy, shoulder-length hair that clung to his sunken cheeks.

"Father Jack!" he repeated.

"Oliver?" Jack asked, surprised at his resourcefulness—or luck—in finding him. "How did you find me?"

The skinny man hunched over, hands on his knees, catching his breath. Once his air replenished, he righted himself and looked at Jack, his dark eyes obscured by the tangles of hair.

"I saw you as you were leaving the security booth, Father Jack."

"I told you, Oliver, I'm not a priest, not in that sense. You don't have to refer to me as Father."

"I'm sorry, Fat–, Jack. And call me Ollie. I hate it when people call me Oliver."

Jack had gotten that impression early on but didn't care. If Oliver was to join his crusade, he would have to adapt to things he found unpleasant, including the sound of his given name.

"If you plan on joining me, I'll refer to you as I please, Oliver."

Ollie's face scrunched with irritation, but he didn't protest. Instead, he asked, "Where are we going?"

Jack looked off in the distance, wondering himself. His first concern had been putting space between himself and the sanitarium. At the moment, the priority was shelter. After that, he would develop a plan to flee the state. There was ample opportunity beyond Illinois to continue his ministry.

"Hey! Don't move!"

A voice came from the left. Then a light blinded them. Jack lifted his forearm to shield his vision and saw Mick, the idiot orderly, brandishing a flashlight and baton. It wasn't standard issue for orderlies to arm themselves, so he must have procured one from the security detail in case he ran into trouble rounding up the escapees.

Jack's own baton was sheathed, and he contemplated if he should reach for it. Mick didn't appear to have a gun, but his weapon was primed to strike while Jack's was holstered. Ollie was useless. Mick wasn't big on brains, but he was strong. He would pummel Ollie, leaving them in a one-on-one fight—a fight Jack wasn't convinced he could win.

He extended his hands, showing he was unarmed. Ollie followed suit.

"That's Bob's uniform, you sick fuck. You did that to him!" Mick spat at the escaped mental patient.

"No, Mick, I found him dead. He didn't need his uniform anymore, so I took it. Wasn't me who killed him."

"Bullshit!" Mick said, stepping forward. "You're going to pay for this!"

Before he could advance farther, something struck him from behind, sending him tumbling forward. The baton slid from his grip upon landing, sliding along the rain-slicked ground. Ollie snatched it as Jack peered into the darkness, looking for the perpetrator.

A large shape emerged from between the trees. As the figure came into view, Jack saw it was Wallace Little, his dark angel. Jack met the big man's eyes, which betrayed a deeper intelligence than his silent demeanor revealed. Jack sensed untapped potential. A smile touched his lips, grateful to the man for preventing their recapture.

Mick tried to get back to his feet, but Ollie met him with an uppercut using the stolen baton. The blow landed with a sickening crack. The impact sent the man crashing backward, mud splattering his head. He coughed hard, spitting up blood and shards of broken teeth.

Jack's smile widened as he approached the downed man, crouching to address him.

"You should have just let us go, Mick," he said. "You would have gotten to go home to your wife tonight."

Mick attempted to rise, pushing off his left hand, but Jack was quicker, standing and stomping on it. "Fuck!" he shouted as Jack ground his foot into Mick's knuckles as if he was stamping out a cigarette.

"You could always renounce this life you lead and follow us. What do you say?"

Mick looked up. Blood spilled from his mouth, mingling with the rain.

"I say go fuck yourself, you psycho."

Jack's grin fell as soon as the words came out. "That's unfortunate." He shifted focus to the large inmate. "How about you, Wallace? Would you like to join me in service to Ba'al?"

Wallace spoke with action, reaching down and grabbing Mick by his collar, lifting him as easily as one would an infant. As Mick's feet dangled off the ground, he panicked and grabbed Wallace's wrists, trying in vain to pry himself free. But the large man was too strong.

To Jack's delight, Wallace carried Mick to a tree with a thick, jagged branch protruding from the trunk. He released the left side of the orderly's collar, keeping control with his right. He pressed his free hand into the man's forehead, guiding him into the branch.

The wood penetrated the man's neck just below his hairline. Jack watched as the skin on the front of Mick's throat stretched then tore as the branch exited, sending a gout of blood splashing onto Wallace's face. The big man registered no emotion as he stepped away, leaving Mick impaled.

The dying man thrashed, trying desperately to extricate himself. His attempts to scream escaped in choked gurgles. Blood seeped from his mouth, pooling in the gaping hole in his jugular.

Ollie laughed at the macabre scene, while Wallace tilted his head like an artist admiring his work. Jack took in the scene and smiled. Despite their inexperience, he believed he could mold them.

It didn't take long for Mick to die. His hands fell limp as they slipped from the branch, coming to a rest on either side of his lifeless body.

Wallace, bloody face washed clean by rain, turned toward Jack. The dark crimson that stained his gown faded into a lighter shade as the water soaked through.

"Does this mean you'll join us?"

Wallace contemplated the offer in silence. After a moment, he nodded, to Jack's delight.

"Excellent! And you, Oliver? I assume you have the stomach for this work?"

Ollie tamped down his annoyance at Jack using his full name. He nodded and said, "I'm with you."

"Then follow me. We have much to do."

CHAPTER 2

Susan Moran blinked the sleep from her eyes as the wipers worked to clear the rain. She gripped the steering wheel at ten and two as the worn-down vehicle puttered down the rural highway.

Her brother's farm in Warren County was one hundred fifty miles from her home. Thanks to the storm, she had been on the road for over three hours. But she had to create as much distance from Woodbury as possible.

A small groan escaped from the back. Susan's son, Franky, was curled on the bench seat, tossing and turning through a restless sleep. The eight-year-old's cherubic features were hidden as his back was toward her.

Seeing her son triggered a resurgent resolve, superseding fatigue.

Susan felt a slight sting on her left forearm. She looked at the deep-purple bruise exposed where the sleeve of her raincoat had slid down. She pulled the yellow nylon over the contusion, hiding the injury, along with the memories.

Charles's face flashed in her mind's eye. It wasn't the ruggedly handsome man she had married shortly after high school. Rather, it was the bitter, violent drunk who routinely made his family surrogates for the world he blamed for his litany of failures, her childhood sweetheart who became a monster.

Susan couldn't pinpoint one specific moment where Charles changed. It was a slow build, starting with bouts of moodiness. Next, she noticed he drank an extra beer after work. Then two. Then three. Before long, she would have to carry him from his recliner to their bedroom most evenings. The worst part was when it gave him a second wind. That resulted in sex that was unsatisfying at best and violative at worst.

But God forbid she shirk her *wifely duties*. Rejecting his advances would prompt a barrage of vile insults.

Bitch. Whore. Cunt.

The man once vowed to love, honor, and cherish her. Now his words dehumanized her.

Susan shouldn't have been surprised when he hit her. But she was.

On the day of Franky's third birthday party, Charles and Susan hosted a backyard barbecue. Limited space indoors meant having guests was only possible if the weather cooperated. Susan's whole family came out to celebrate. Even Charles's father made the drive from Barrington.

The party started off well. Charles looked genuinely

happy at the grill, slinging burgers and hot dogs. He was cordial with her family and even ran around the yard in a circle with Franky seated on his shoulders, arms outstretched, pretending to be an airplane. That sweet, toddler giggle was music to her ears.

During the singing of *Happy Birthday*, Susan noticed Charles sounded different. The memory sickened her, eliciting the same gut-wrenching tightness now. His speech, thick with slurring, signaled worse to come.

Worse came once their guests departed. Charles had plopped himself on his recliner with a fresh beer, having crossed double digits.

Susan did her best to keep it together, but she was tired. As the event wound down, the idea of tidying and returning the house to its normal state seemed daunting. She could've waited until morning, but that would irritate Charles. She cleaned while managing her cranky toddler, whose whines were exacerbated by sugar and exhaustion.

So there she was, washing her husband's grill utensils while Franky slammed his new toys about. The siren of the fire truck Charles's dad gave him was especially grating. She spared a glance toward her husband and observed his face twist in irritation.

Wanting to avoid his ire, Susan haphazardly tossed a dish towel on the counter as she moved toward her child, inadvertently knocking over a beer bottle. It clinked as it toppled onto the granite surface. For a split second, she registered relief, but the bottle rolled off the counter. Susan was too slow to catch it. It crashed to the linoleum, shattering on impact. Susan yelped and jumped back as shards of glass sprayed. She snatched Franky up, and the startled boy yowled.

Susan feared her husband, but she hadn't reached the point where she couldn't express herself. She foresaw a flood of obscenities and vitriol resulting from her audacity. But exhaustion and frustration prevented discretion.

"Goddamn it, Charles! Can you please help me here?"

She regretted the words as soon as they left her mouth. Not because she was wrong to be frustrated, but because she feared retaliation. It didn't matter. She said the words. She had to own them.

Charles's reaction was not explosive. For a moment, she thought perhaps she got through to him. Maybe he saw his wife struggling and his child crying and recognized their need for help.

The hue of his face, as red as the firetruck, said otherwise. His eyes burned with intensity as he rose from the chair.

Susan knew she wasn't in the wrong, but her words didn't comport with her feelings. They were a meek, whispered plea.

"I'm sorry ..."

Charles responded with a slap.

That first impact didn't hurt. It was more of a sudden pressure on her cheek. She tightened her grip on Franky, whose screams had increased in vociferousness. While she focused on not dropping her child, the stinging set in and her eyes watered.

She righted her head and was met with another slap. That time, the pain was instant, causing her to bite her lower lip. Her ears rang from the jolt as she tasted the coppery tinge of blood.

"Watch your fucking mouth, bitch," Charles spat. "I'll put you through a fucking wall."

Susan was stunned. Her husband had struck her—twice. Should she hit him back? She couldn't hurt him. Call the police? Good luck with that. Plunge a butcher knife into his throat? Every imaginable emotion coursed through her, stirring a wave of nausea, making her feel like she may lose her balance. She pulled Franky tighter, the toddler screaming into her shoulder, tears and spittle soaking her shirt.

Susan opened her mouth to say something, unsure of what. Charles raised his hand, which was no longer open. It was clenched in a fist.

"If the next word out of your mouth isn't 'I understand,' I'll break your fucking jaw."

"I ...I ...I ..."

His knuckles whitened.

"You fucking what?"

"I understand," she choked out, the words stinging worse than her cheek, a betrayal of her dignity.

Charles unclenched the fist, and the redness faded from his face. He tilted his head, considering her while she trembled under him. His focus stayed on her, but he raised his open hand again, slowly and gently. He patted Franky's head. Despite not seeing who touched him, the boy recoiled on instinct, and Charles withdrew his hand as if burned.

Susan saw the tsunami of rage rise again, along with the crimson flush of his skin. She wanted to flee, but fear paralyzed her. Her feet may as well have been fused to the floor.

Standing in fear before the man she loved, she watched him relax his posture and breathe a heavy sigh, the color again draining back to a normal shade. He reached his hand back up to Franky's head. Thankfully, the boy didn't resist while his father ruffled his hair. He leaned in and gave his son a kiss on the cheek.

"Happy birthday, buddy." He turned back to Susan. "I'll see you upstairs."

Charles had one last statement to make. He swiped his arm across the counter, sending beer bottles, utensils, and the remnants of Franky's birthday cake crashing to the floor. Her grandmother's decorative crystal cake dish exploded on impact, along with more bottles. Franky screamed again. Susan stifled her own.

Susan needed five years to muster the courage to break free as her marriage shattered like the glass did that night. The memory of that moment brought a fresh phantom sting to the weary woman's cheek. She had been struck so many times since then that the sensation became as familiar as brushing her teeth. The resolve to never let it happen again intensified, along with her grip on the steering wheel.

Susan looked back at Franky, hearing him moan again in his sleep.

The boy tossed and turned in a restless slumber. Susan was angered at the sight of the purple that had formed across the lower part of the boy's jaw in the hours since his father struck him.

The first time Charles raised his hand to Franky was the final straw.

A simple Lego block was the culprit. Franky unknowingly dropped it, and Charles, late for work and hung over, stepped on it with his bare foot, his reaction apoplectic.

Charles stormed into the boy's room as Susan chased, pleading with him to understand it was accidental. He disregarded his wife, grabbing the whimpering child by his shirt and yanking him to his feet.

"You lazy little shit!"

Franky cowered.

"I'm sorry, Daddy! Why are you mad? I'm sorry!"

His father responded with a slap. Point made, he released his grip on Franky's shirt, and the stunned child fell hard on his bottom. The impact exacerbated the boy's pain. The pain intensified his fear.

Charles didn't show a hint of remorse. If Susan had a weapon, she would have ended him right there. But despite her boiling hatred for her husband, she remained calm. It was her only chance to protect her son in this powder keg situation.

As he left the room, Charles addressed his wife in a calm yet menacing tone. "Clean this fucking house by the time I get home."

Fifteen minutes later, Susan remained cradling her son on his bed. His cries had faded to whimpers, and the tears had slowed to a trickle. She watched as Charles walked by the door, the sunlight from the open windows glinting off the olive-colored leather of his

Woodbury Sheriff's Department jacket. The uniform itself was a mockery.

To serve and protect. Bullshit.

Charles shook his head with disdain as he passed his family.

The door opened and closed moments later. Susan rushed to the window, watching as the police cruiser drove off. She stood there for over twenty minutes, fearful Charles would return, having forgotten his wallet or, maybe, just to abuse them more.

After a brief call to her brother, Kevin, she sprang to action. It wasn't long before she was on the road, with Franky in the backseat, vowing to leave Woodbury and her boogeyman behind forever.

After what seemed like eternity, Susan finally saw a clearing. Relief set in as her brother's farm emerged through the still-torrential downpour.

The modest farmhouse was weathered, with a large wraparound porch and wood siding. Despite the remoteness, the glow of electric light emanated from within. Several outbuildings framed the exterior behind the barn and chicken coop. A toolshed, hidden by the downpour, sat toward the back of the property.

Kevin didn't have animals on his farm. His primary output was corn and soybeans. Susan wished she had opted for that kind of simpler life. Not that farming wasn't hard—she knew Kevin worked his ass off—but years of suburban living only got her used and abused. Thankfully, she wouldn't encounter people like that here.

Susan parked next to Kevin's worn-out yet still-functional pickup. Franky climbed into the front seat and huddled close as she opened the door. She used her raincoat to shield her son as she bounded up the stairs.

Her brother waited for her, standing to one side of the open doorway, ushering them in. Susan was barely inside when she flung her arms around him, pulling him in tight. Tears flowed freely as she found comfort in her sibling. Kevin welcomed the embrace, caring little that she was soaking wet.

"It's okay, Suse. You're safe now."

CHAPTER 3

"**R**eally? Out of gas?"

Vic Fannelli offered his girlfriend an apologetic look. "It had more than half a tank! I swear!"

Ashley Harris wasn't buying it. If her scowl wasn't enough to convey her dissatisfaction with her beau, her stiff posture and crossed arms drove the point home. Or it *should* have, but in doing so, she pushed her breasts together, drawing Vic's focus—and not in the way she wanted. Sure, she enjoyed the way his jaw dropped when he saw her Barbarella costume, but sitting in a stalled car in the middle of nowhere, during a damn rainstorm to boot, she was less than enthused.

"Uh huh," Ashley muttered. "Driving all the way out here to your buddy Rick's farm party was your idea. Now we *conveniently* run out of gas in fucking no-man's-land? Right." The drawn-out last word showcased her sarcasm. She looked away.

"Babe, I'm not lying. The stupid gas gauge is busted

or something! Why would I want to break down on the side of the road? Out here of all places?"

Ashley kept her eyes focused ahead, not wanting her anger to soften at how cute Vic looked in his Tony Manero *Saturday Night Fever* costume. So what if he wasn't John Travolta? Who was?

Vic was no slouch in the looks department. He wasn't a Rhodes Scholar, but he was funny and, dare she admit, even charming. Deep down, she knew this wasn't some elaborate set-up. The weather, long drive, and now car trouble combined to put her in a foul mood, all for a stupid party she hadn't even wanted to attend.

And Vic found himself in the unfortunate position of being the only one toward which she could point her ire.

"You're just trying to make me put out!"

Vic laughed as he ran his hands through his perfectly coiffed hair. "We have sex all the time! Why go through all this trouble?"

"Because you're a pervert! "

Vic laughed again. "Well, yeah. I'm not denying that."

That made Ashley laugh. She gave in and looked at Vic, that stupid smirk disarming her almost instantly. "Well, you're still not getting any."

Vic protruded his lips in an exaggerated pout. "What else are we going to do?"

"I knew it! You asshole!" She slapped Vic's arm.

"Hey!" Vic rubbed the impact area in mock pain through the white polyester material of his jacket. "I didn't plan this, but that doesn't mean we can't seize the opportunity."

"Or you can seize the opportunity to take your ass down the road to find some gas."

Vic cocked a surprised eyebrow. "In this weather? There isn't a gas station for miles. We're better off waiting until it stops."

Ashley gestured at the rain-battered window. "Does this look like it's stopping anytime soon?"

"No," Vic said, sitting back. "You don't expect me to leave you alone here while I stumble around on the off chance that I find gas do you?"

"Ugh!" Ashley blurted, throwing up her hands.

"Plus, I'm pretty sure there are coyotes out there."

Awkward silence hung between the couple for a few minutes. Vic tapped the steering wheel. Even if it wasn't an elaborate ruse in his perpetual quest for nookie, he still fucked up. Ashley again crossed her arms while her leg jackhammered up and down. Vic reached over and placed his hand on Ashley's knee, using a firm but gentle touch to halt the restless bouncing. She met his eyes, seeing the genuine remorse in them.

"Hey," Vic said, "I'm sorry. I didn't mean for this to happen. The gauge is busted. For real."

She nodded, then said, "So, what do we do?"

Vic craned his neck, assessing how far down the road he could see. "Someone's gotta drive by at some point."

Ashley glanced down the road, then toward the rear window. Nothing. "You sure about that?" she asked.

"Not a lot of choice. Worst case, we'll wait for the

rain to stop, then hoof it to a gas station."

Neither option was great. Everything about the scenario felt wrong. It felt like an ominous presence moved among the raindrops, hiding just beyond sight.

Vic sensed her apprehension and gave her hand a gentle squeeze. "I'll get us home," he said. "And I'll make it up to you. Honest."

She lightened. "Damn right you will!" She held out her left ring finger. "This whole scenario just cost you *at least* an extra karat—if you ever decide to propose, that is."

Vic looked sad; Ashley had hit a nerve. After four years together, she thought marriage was their future. Still, raising the topic at that moment wasn't appropriate.

"I just want it to be perfect." Vic's voice was soft, a hair above a whisper.

She chuckled, putting her hand on the back of his head and running her fingers through his dark hair. "Probably not the best time."

She pulled him toward her for a kiss, a peace offering. As she pulled back, a tap on Vic's window surprised them.

A uniformed man stood outside their car, baton in hand. To Vic, he looked like a police officer. He was drenched yet unbothered. He twirled his hand, signaling Vic to roll down the window.

Ashley looked back for a police car. There wasn't one. Maybe it was hidden in the dark. But no lights? Wasn't that standard protocol for cops helping stranded motorists? She almost warned Vic against lowering the window but was too late.

"Car trouble?"

"Um, yes, sir. Out of gas."

The cop laughed. "Out of gas! Damn, boy, how stupid you gotta be to run out of gas out here?"

Vic offered an awkward chuckle. "Yes, sir. That was pretty dumb of me." The man, observing the couple, didn't acknowledge the admission, so Vic posed a question of his own. "Can you help us?"

"Sure can! Why don't you step out of the car and we'll take a look?"

"Where's your car?" Ashley said before Vic could comply.

The cop looked behind him. "Oh, just a ways down the road. Come on out and we'll make a run for it."

"Why can't you just bring it here? I'd rather my girlfriend not to have to run through the rain."

The man disliked that reply. "Boy, are you disobeying an officer of the law?"

"No, I'm just—"

"Just running off at your mouth. Get out of the car."

"Sir, I'm only asking—"

"I don't give two shits what you're asking, son. Get out of the damn car."

Ashley squeezed Vic's arm, silently urging him not to. As she did, she glimpsed the emblem on the man's jacket—Pine Hill Security. She felt a shiver up her spine.

"He's not a cop," she whispered.

Vic rolled up the window. The man didn't intervene.

Ashley thought he may walk away, but the man's baton shattered the window, dispelling the notion. The couple raised their arms and screamed as the shards showered them.

The man stepped aside, and a larger man emerged. A sopping-wet hospital gown clung to his bulky frame. The bigger man disengaged the lock and pulled the door open. Vic tried to stop him, but the guy was too strong. He grabbed Vic and tossed him, sending him slamming hard to the asphalt.

"Vic!" Ashley screamed as she lunged forward. She hesitated, debating between escaping or shutting the door.

She never got to make that choice. A third, skinnier man, wearing a similar gown, grabbed her hair and yanked her out too. The man, who was stronger than he looked, wrapped his arms around her torso, trapping her in a reverse bear hug.

As she screamed, the others stood over Vic, who was trying to recover. Her panic reached its apex as she struggled. When she felt the skinny man's body reacting to hers, revulsion entered the mix.

The big man stomped on Vic's lower back, and Ashley heard him choke as the breath fled from his lungs. The police imposter crouched in front of him. He slid his baton under her boyfriend's chin, raising his head so he could look him in the eye.

The man studied Vic before letting his head drop. Fearful of continued violence, Vic remained still. The man rose, eyes on Ashley.

She stopped struggling and sobbed, begging for their lives. "Please, don't hurt us."

The man approached, getting close enough that she

felt his hot, stale breath wash over her. "You are both heretics, unworthy to serve. However, that doesn't mean you can't serve a purpose."

She wasn't sure what that meant. Whatever purpose he was referring to couldn't be a good one.

The man walked back toward Vic, arms outstretched as he shouted to the sky. "Great and powerful Ba'al, I offer this sacrifice in your honor."

Realization washed over Ashley, and she unleashed a tortured scream before the first strike.

Vic raised his head as far as he could, but the baton crashed into it, sending a gout of blood spouting from the point of impact. A sickening crunch accompanied his head smacking back against the ground. The baton rose and fell. The sound transitioned from cracking to squishing mush as the maniac destroyed the skull of Ashley's love.

When the assault ended, the man righted his posture and stretched. The rain diluted and washed Vic's blood from the baton.

He called to the sky. "Lord Ba'al, accept this sacrifice in your name!"

Ashley's screams echoed as Vic's blood mingled with the puddle beneath his twitching body.

The man offered a sadistic smile as he approached. She struggled anew, but the skinny man held strong. Vic's killer stepped in front of her, flanked by his larger companion. As with Vic, he thrust the nightstick under her chin, pushing her head back. The skinny man again shuddered behind her while he took a generous whiff of her soaking-wet hair.

The leader addressed him.

"Oliver," he said, "you seem distracted by this one."

"I'm sorry, Father Jack," Oliver said, his inflection like a scolded child. "She's just... so damn pretty. I ain't seen a woman like her in a long time. Got me feeling all types of things."

Jack observed Ashley.

She implored him with her eyes. *Don't let him do this.* The plea went unanswered.

"I need you focused on the tasks ahead, Oliver. You may have five minutes, no more. Do with her as you wish."

She felt Oliver's sinister smile as his grip tightened. Ashley screamed as the skinny psychopath dragged her away.

CHAPTER 4

Charles Moran found himself getting irritated as he turned down his street. A shitty end to a shitty day. Woodbury's lack of excitement was, in fact, its defining characteristic. Nothing ever happened there. Being a law enforcement officer in their quiet burg was akin to working as a security guard at an abandoned warehouse. During patrols, dealing with occasional drunkenness, disorderly conduct, or property disputes was part of the job, but most of his days were spent cruising around, drinking coffee, eating donuts, and slowly expanding his waistline.

As he got closer to home, he daydreamed about how he should have moved out west instead of letting himself get stuck in this rinky-dink town. He could have learned to surf and married a blonde beach bunny. That would have been better than being stuck where he was with a nagging wife and bratty kid.

Goddamn, they pissed him off this morning. All

Franky had to do was clean up after himself. It wasn't like he was still in diapers. The damn kid was eight, more than old enough to learn some responsibility. Part of him felt bad for hitting his son, but what else was he supposed to do? His mother babied him like some helpless, wounded deer. What she didn't realize was that wounded animals didn't survive. The thought of his son being that weak sickened Charles. That was why it was on him to toughen the boy up. And Susan wasn't going to stand in his way.

Still, he probably shouldn't have smacked the kid; he could have gotten the point across by yelling. Charles knew he went too far sometimes. He just couldn't help it. Once his vision turned red, he couldn't calm himself, no matter how much he tried. But Susan never saw him try. She only saw him fail. Just like everyone else.

The sheriff was no different. Charles worked hard, but Sheriff Freeman promoted Jim Curtis to deputy over him. It was only because they were hunting buddies. It had nothing to do with who was the better cop, because that was Charles. No doubt in his mind.

Deep down, he knew it wasn't his family's fault, just like he knew he shouldn't have hit Franky. He wouldn't outright apologize, but maybe he would go in and act like nothing happened. He was sure he made his point.

The idea that Charles's homecoming would be conciliatory vanished when he approached the house and saw the car was gone. The Moran family only owned one—well, they would own it after twenty-some more payments—but one of the few perks of the job was Charles being able to take his cruiser home. But the family car should have been there. Susan hadn't told him she would be going out, especially not at that hour when she should be making dinner.

Where the fuck is she?

Charles sped up rather than slowed as he pulled into the driveway, bottoming out before coming to a screeching stop.

He rushed inside, already expecting what he would find before he actually saw it. He checked Franky's room first. Drawers had been haphazardly left open, as was the closet door. Not all of his son's clothes were gone, but enough of them were missing to confirm his suspicions. A similar scene met him in the master bedroom.

The bitch really ran out on him, and she took his son with her.

But his darling wife wasn't as clever as she thought. There was only one place she could go. Her mom died two years ago, and her father was in a nursing home. That only left her brother, Kevin. His farm was out in Warren County, not far from the Pine Hill looney bin.

Charles felt the anger bubbling up as he thought about the hundred-fifty-mile drive to his brother-in-law's farm. He had been working all day, and now Susan was forcing him to drive for the next two-and-a-half hours just to bring her ungrateful ass home. Not to mention there was a doozy of a storm in the forecast.

If she thought that last beating was bad, she better just wait. And if Kevin interjected himself into his business with his wife, then Charles would teach him a lesson too.

He didn't even bother to change out of his uniform as he got into his car and went to bring his family home.

CHAPTER 5

When Susan finally broke the hug, she dried her eyes and observed her surroundings. The farm itself was small, but the residence was spacious. The wood floors were weathered and chipped but sturdy. A large area rug covered the space between the couch and the small stand where a thirteen-inch television sat, unused. Kevin had mentioned it was difficult to get a signal out there, and with the rain, it must be damn near impossible. Maybe one day there would be better technology to broadcast to more remote areas, but for the time being, they were at the mercy of the rabbit ears. A jack-o'-lantern with a friendly but somehow still creepy smile rested on the table next to the window to the right of the door. A small glow emanated from inside the carved pumpkin.

With the open floor plan of the house, the dining room was visible from Susan's vantage point in the entryway. The circular oak table was large enough to seat ten, and the hutch against the wall on the opposite side proudly displayed her sister-in-law's ceramic dinnerware. Debra had once told Susan that her grandmother had left her the set when she passed. It was one of the few things she had to remember her.

Speaking of Debra, she was seated at the dining room table, going through some pamphlets and scattered papers. Susan noticed the cross emblem on the pamphlet's cover. Debra had become more engrossed in her faith recently. She had always been a churchgoer, as was Susan's brother, but Susan had noticed a gradual change over the past year or so.

Debra was never one to dress provocatively, but now she seemed to be a step below Puritanical. Knee-length skirts had transitioned to ankle length, and every button on her shirt was fastened up to the neck. She hadn't even worn a bathing suit to the lake when they visited over the summer. She just sat in a chair on the dock, fully clothed, fanning herself, while Kevin swam with the kids.

Susan wondered how her brother felt about his wife's new demeanor. Did her prudishness make its way to their bedroom? Not that Susan wanted to think about her brother's sex life, but she knew how Charles reacted whenever he didn't get his way in bed. But she couldn't imagine Kevin being like that. If he was, she wouldn't have come here. Still, it had to be frustrating. Regardless, their marriage always seemed solid, so whatever their arrangement, it clearly worked for them. And Susan was in no position to cast aspersions.

She sniffled and cleared her throat before greeting her sister-in-law.

"Hi, Deb."

Debra looked up from her work but didn't come over to greet her. "Hello, Susan. Please, make yourself at home."

The greeting was friendly enough, but something about it lacked warmth. It made Susan feel like an inconvenience. That missing affection was found when she addressed Franky, who was standing close to his mother, clinging to the damp fabric of her jeans. "Oh my, Franky! You've gotten so big since the last time we saw you! You must be eating your vegetables!"

"Ew," Franky whispered.

Debra chuckled and got out of the chair, making her way to the staircase on the opposite side of the room. She craned her head around so she could shout up to the second floor.

"Kids! Aunt Susan and Cousin Franky are here! Come down and say hi!" She started to walk away, but a thought must have entered her mind because she turned back. "And Molly Green, that bedroom door better be *wide* open!"

An exasperated but muffled groan from the upper level preceded the creak of an old door opening. Debra rolled her eyes and shot Kevin a disapproving glare before shouting back in an icy tone. "*Thank you.*"

She finally came over to Susan and put an arm on her shoulder. Her expression was sympathetic but, as with her initial greeting, seemed somehow artificial. It felt like pity seasoned with a smattering of judgment.

Kevin had done his best to get along with Charles in the early days. They were never particularly close, but they kept it cordial. Debra, on the other hand, never liked her brother-in-law. As his behavior worsened, so did Deb's disdain. She probably thought Susan was weak for putting up with it for all those years.

Let she without sin cast the first stone, Susan thought. It irritated her further because she couldn't find any *sins* to speak of when it came to her brother's wife. But she wasn't about to get into a snipping contest with the woman who was opening her home to a family in need.

"Thank you for letting us stay here," Susan said. "I promise it won't be long. I just have to figure out what we're going to do."

"It's no bother," Debra said. "You're welcome to stay as long as you need. Right, Kevin?"

"Of course," Kevin said with a nod. He looked like he wanted to ask a million questions to understand what happened but didn't want to do so in front of Franky. He crouched to address his nephew, ruffling his hair. It reminded Susan of how Charles had done the same on that horrible night after the party. Only when Kevin did it, there was genuine affection. "Hey, kiddo, you must be pretty tired. But Annie is going to be so excited to see you!"

"Franky!" A small girl's voice heralded Annie Green's arrival as she came thumping down the stairs. Also eight years old, Annie was small, with a fair complexion. A mix of her parents, she inherited Kevin's blue eyes but her mother's dark hair. Contrasting Debra, however, was her genuine enthusiasm at seeing her cousin. She ran over to him and grabbed his hand. "Want to play hide and seek?"

"How about we let Franky get changed and settled before you two run off?" Debra said.

"Okay," Annie said with sing-song disappointment.

A creak on the floorboards in the direction of the kitchen drew Debra's attention, and she called back without looking. "I think you two had quite enough at dinner."

"C'mon, Mom," Tim Green whined as he entered from the kitchen, carrying a plate of chocolate chip cookies and a glass of milk. "That was like an hour ago."

While Annie had characteristics of both her parents, thirteen-year-old Tim was the spitting image of Kevin, from the sandy hue of his hair to the slight downturn of his nose. It was like looking into a time capsule every time Susan saw him. There was another boy with him. He looked to be about the same age but was short and stout when compared to her nephew's taller, lankier build. His dark, shaggy hair hung down over his forehead, almost to the point of obscuring his eyes.

"And you're going to load up on candy tomorrow night. I don't see any reason for you to gorge yourself on cookies now."

"But Mom ..."

"But nothing. You can each have *one*. And maybe not be so rude and say hello to your aunt and cousin."

"Hi, Aunt Suse," Tim said. "Hi, Franky."

Franky waved, saying nothing.

Susan said, "Hi, Tim, nice to see you."

Debra gave her son a glare, offering a silent instruction. It took Tim a second to get the hint.

"Oh, yeah." He gestured to the other boy. "This is my friend, Mikey. He's sleeping over tonight. We were going to watch scary movies, but the TV isn't working."

"Hopefully it's back for Doctor Dementia tomorrow! Six straight hours of horror movies! It's going to be so cool!"

Horror movies are cool until you live one, Susan thought. "Well, that sounds great, Mikey. Nice to meet you."

"Yeah, you too!"

Tim nudged his friend, hoping that somehow his mother may have forgotten her directive to only have one cookie each, as they started toward the stairs.

"Eh em."

Tim stopped and turned back to the kitchen with a resigned sigh, gesturing for Mikey to follow him. The shorter boy followed dutifully.

The middle and youngest child accounted for, Debra again called to her oldest, a new level of irritation permeating her tone. "Molly!"

"Jesus, Mom, I'm right here! You don't have to shout." Molly was halfway down the stairs when Debra had yelled to her. At eighteen years old, she was the oldest of Kevin's children, and the biggest handful. Whereas her mother's dress was modest, bordering on prudish, Molly favored more trendy clothing like crop tops and bell-bottom jeans, a style she was rocking at the present moment and, judging by Debra's expression, one her mother disapproved of.

A tall, handsome boy not much older than Molly followed behind her. He wore a plaid, button-down shirt underneath his overalls, one strap of which hung loosely down to his waistline.

"If I have to call you three times, I'm going to shout. And don't take the Lord's name in vain."

Molly subtly rolled her eyes and came up to Susan, embracing her in a warm hug. "Hey, Aunt Suse," she said.

Susan hugged her back. Sure, the girl could be snarky and often saw rules as little more than suggestions, but she was always genuinely kind to her aunt. Any minor irritations she presented to her parents weren't serious in the grand scheme of things. Susan always saw her as a free spirit. She was young and adventurous and looking to get the most out of life. Now, more so than ever, those were qualities Susan could appreciate.

When they broke the hug, Susan looked at the young man beside her. She didn't have to prompt as Molly offered the introduction.

"This is George. George McBride. He's my... friend."

Her hesitation at the title wasn't lost on Susan, especially seeing the way Debra glared a hole into them. Using the word *boyfriend* may have been a bit too much for an overbearing mother to hear. But Debra wasn't stupid.

"Oh, please," Debra said. "Like I don't know you two are dating. You're eighteen, Molly, you're allowed to date. I just don't want you behind closed bedroom doors in my house. Is that too much to ask?"

"No, ma'am," George answered innocently. "I

totally understand. My folks would say the same thing." He turned his attention to Susan and offered a hand, parroting Molly's introduction. "Hello, Ms. Green, I'm George. George McBride."

Susan took his hand and shook it, not bothering to correct him on her name. In fact, it occurred to her for the first time she thought she wanted to go back to her maiden name, maybe even fill out the paperwork to change Franky's too. The thought of wearing her monster of a husband's surname suddenly felt repulsive to her.

"Nice to meet you, George."

George smiled politely. "Are there any bags you need help with? I'd be happy to run out and get them for you."

"Thank you, sweetie, but it can wait until the rain stops."

"No, ma'am, y'all look like you need to get into some dry clothes. I'll be in and out before the rain gets me too bad." He held out his hand again, this time to request the car keys.

Susan smiled gratefully and handed them to him. "It's just two bags. They're in the trunk. Thank you so much."

"My pleasure," George said, taking the keys and breaking into a jog before he was even out the door.

Susan gave Molly a raised eyebrow signaling her approval and mouthed the words, *He's cute.*

Molly giggled and nodded, as amused as Debra was annoyed.

"They're all polite until they're trying to stuff their

hand down your pants."

"Mom!"

Even Kevin didn't look happy about the quip. He didn't say anything, but he did shoot his wife a look to let her know that was uncalled for.

She clearly didn't agree, but she didn't protest, either. She said, "Make yourself at home, Susan." With that, she returned to her pamphlets.

Kevin offered an apologetic half-smile. "You and Franky can stay as long as you like. You can see we have a full house here, but we have plenty of room." He paused before adding, "We can talk about other things whenever you're ready."

Susan squeezed his arm. "Thanks, big bro. This means a lot. More than you know."

Before the siblings could get mushier, George came running in, dripping wet despite his best efforts to dodge the rain. He was holding the two suitcases Susan had hurriedly packed before getting on the road. "Where should I put these, Mr. Green?"

Kevin gestured upstairs. "The guest room across from the bathroom will do." He turned to Susan. "There's a queen bed in there for you and Franky to share." Back to George. "Thanks, bud. You can bring them up."

Molly rushed over and grabbed the smaller of the suitcases. "I can get Franky's," she explained. "I'll make sure you get them in the right room." The young couple started upstairs.

Debra, of course, gave them a warning before they departed. "Doors open."

"Yes, ma'am," George said.

Annie tugged at Susan's sleeve to get her attention. "Can you guys get changed now so Franky and I can play?"

Mikey sat down on the bed, munching the last of the sole cookie he had been allowed, as Tim closed the door to the bedroom, having wolfed down his own on the way upstairs.

"Your mom makes pretty good cookies," Mikey noted. "Too bad she's so damn stingy with them."

"Hurry up and eat that," Tim instructed. "We got shit to do."

Mikey was confused. He looked out the window at the rain that showed no signs of stopping. "We're not still going out in this, are we?"

"Of course we are," Tim answered incredulously. "It's fucking Mischief Night. This has been the plan for weeks."

"Yeah, but I didn't know it'd be raining like this. I think I saw a damn rowboat float by out there."

"Oh, what, you going to melt? Just because your mom flies around on a broom doesn't mean you'll disintegrate if you get wet."

"You really want to talk about mothers?"

"Stop deflecting, man. You knew all along that tonight was going to be the night we got back at Mr. Wilbur. He has to pay."

"Yeah, but—"

"But nothing, Mikey! The old man moves in for two weeks and he thinks he can just tear down my treehouse?"

"I mean, it did end up being his property."

"Fuck that!" Tim was pissed. "It was right on the edge of his property. It ain't like he's growing anything there. He did it just to be an asshole."

"I guess."

Tim put on a raincoat and pulled a small shoebox from under his bed. He opened it and smiled as he inspected the contents. "And someone has to teach that asshole a lesson."

CHAPTER 6

Dick Wilbur polished off his third glass of Wild Turkey and barely spared a second before pouring another. Neither the booze nor the fire he sat in front of chased the chill from his body. He didn't even know why he bothered with the glass. He was going to kill the damn bottle anyway. Dick guessed in some warped way that if he didn't drink straight from the bottle, he wasn't an alcoholic even though he knew he was. It had been a long time since he woke up hangover-free. He certainly hadn't in the two years since Ellie passed.

His wife was fifty-two years old when she dropped dead of a heart attack at their kitchen table. No warning. No nothing. She didn't smoke and rarely drank, just a glass of wine with dinner once in a while. She wasn't obese and had no history of heart disease in her family. But just like that, she ended up face down in a plate of spaghetti after her ticker gave out.

Dick couldn't stay in their home in Woodbury after

that. How could he eat dinner at that table knowing his wife had died there during dinner on a random Wednesday evening? No, he sold that place as soon as he could, taking quite the hit on the price. He bought this shithole farmhouse at auction for probably half its value. Sure, it needed work, but it wasn't nothing Dick couldn't handle himself. If he ever got around to it.

The place was perfect because it got him away from everyone. Without his Ellie, he had no desire to pretend to socialize or play nice. He just wanted to sit by himself somewhere quiet and wait to join his darling. The property was small and next to another larger functioning farm, but the actual residence was almost a quarter mile away, so he didn't have to risk exchanging banal pleasantries whenever he stepped out on his porch.

The family had stopped by to say hello the day after he moved in. The wife brought him a plate of chocolate chip cookies. They had three kids. The oldest and youngest were girls, and the middle one was a boy. The two older ones looked like trouble, albeit for different reasons, but Dick kept that to himself. He didn't want to be friends with those folks, but he didn't want to piss them off, either. Not that he cared what they thought of him, he just didn't have the time nor inclination to feud with his neighbors.

He accepted the plate and suffered through a five-minute chat with the couple, whose names escaped him the moment he heard them. Kelvin and Donna or something. When they finally left, he said a silent prayer—despite his grievances with God—that he would never have an interaction with them longer than that. The cookies were good, though.

The thing that really turned Dick off from wanting to engage with them was the kids. There was a time when he and Ellie wanted a bunch of their own. Before they were married, they had said they wanted at least four. But when they failed to conceive despite trying for three years, they wondered if even one would be in the equation. Months of doctor's visits confirmed it wasn't. And it was Ellie that couldn't have children because of some genetic issue she never knew about until they tried.

She was devastated and told Dick she would understand if he left her. She knew he wanted kids and deserved to be with someone that could give him a child. Dick told her he would hear none of that. She was all he needed, and they were all each other had until the day she died. Even though he carried no regret about the twenty-nine years he had spent with his wife, the fact that they never had children of their own always pained him to the point where he didn't even want to be around them.

That was why when he found the boy had a treehouse practically on his property line, he was decidedly less than enthused. He decided to check on it and was actually surprised to see the survey showed the tree did cross onto his property.

He offered Green a chance to take it down himself. At first, his neighbor tried to reach a compromise, emphasizing how much his son loved that treehouse and that he had built it for him before he was even born.

Dick didn't want to hear nothing. He wanted it off his property so he could keep the kid far away. He told Green he could feel free to build another one on the opposite end of the property.

Stubborn, Green refused, forcing Dick to file a complaint with the city, leaving his neighbor no choice but to comply.

That was last month, and they hadn't spoken since, which was just fine with Dick.

The fire was dying, so he grabbed the poker resting on the side of his recliner and used it to push the logs about, stoking the flames. He would have to throw another log in, but he didn't feel like getting up yet. He put his glass to his lips, anticipating the burn of the cheap liquor.

Just as he got the slightest of sips, there was a knock at his door. At first, he wasn't sure it was real. His head was fuzzy from the booze, and besides, who the hell would be there at that hour in that kind of weather? Green had no business there, and there was certainly no help Dick could offer *Mr. High and Mighty Know-it-All.* He hesitated, taking another slow sip while waiting to see if there would be another knock.

Just when he thought it had been in his head, another, louder, knock came from the door.

Goddamn it.

Dick got up with some effort, his bones crackling as he struggled out of the chair. He stole another drink before resting the glass on the table and ambling over to answer. He didn't immediately open it, instead pulling back the curtain of the window next to the door and peering outside.

The man on his porch, standing under the overhang to shield himself from the downpour, was wearing a uniform. It didn't look like a cop. Security, maybe? But what the hell would a security guard be doing out there?

Dick kept the chain fastened as he cracked the door to see what the man wanted. Just as he surmised, the patch on the guard's jacket read Pine Hill Security.

Pine Hill—the looney bin down the road. Another reason he guessed he got the place so cheap.

The security guard smiled when he saw the door open. "Evening, sir."

"Evening," Dick replied. "Can I help you?"

"Maybe, sir. You see, now I don't want to alarm you, but there's been a breakout."

"A breakout?"

"Yessir. At Pine Hill." He pointed to the patch on his jacket.

"What's that got to do with me?"

"Well, sir, these escapees are a dangerous lot. We're searching the area, and I was wondering if you'd give me permission to inspect the premises?"

"Like, in the house?"

"Yessir."

"There isn't anyone here other than me. You're welcome to look around the outside of the property, but you ain't coming in. Have a good evening."

Dick went to close the door, but the man stuck his foot in the crack, preventing him from doing so. He slid the end of a baton through the opening, showing that he was armed.

"Now, sir, someone may have gotten in without you knowing. Or maybe you're hiding one from us?"

"That's absurd. Listen, friend, I don't know what you're after, but it isn't here. Now get your foot out of my door and get the hell off my property before I make you leave."

"You can't speak to an officer of the law like that."

"You ain't no law."

Dick had enough, but he needed his own protection. He could get his rifle, but that was up in his bedroom. Looking around, he saw an acceptable alternative, walking over and grabbing the poker from next to his chair. He approached the door where the man in the security guard's outfit still stood propping it with his foot. He led with the sharp instrument, letting the intruder know he was serious.

Just before he could get to the door, a bolt of lightning streaked the sky, followed by a roaring clap of thunder. As the sound crescendoed, the room went dark, further disorienting Dick's alcohol-dulled senses. His head spun and he felt unsteady as the man kicked the door in, easily breaking the flimsy chain.

Dick raised the poker, but the man didn't give him a chance to use it as he slugged Dick in the chin with his baton. It sent him crashing back into his recliner and over it, sending the chair toppling to the floor. On impact, he lost his grip on the poker, which slid across the floor and into the fireplace, the flames crackling on contact with the iron.

Dick tried to get up but was met by a kick to the

chest from someone else he couldn't see clearly. He must have entered in the darkness. The new assailant stepped into the firelight, and Dick could see he was a smaller, skinnier man wearing a disco suit that looked about two sizes too big.

He tasted blood. He turned to his side and spit a gob onto the floor, splattering the old area rug that had been there when he moved in.

"What the hell do you freaks want?"

The first man, the one in the security guard uniform, crouched over him. "Just somewhere to get out of the rain."

"Why didn't you just ask me that?"

"Oh, come now. You weren't going to let us in."

"Well, you're here now. So stay." He coughed, bringing up more blood. "You can stay here."

The man stood. "We intend to. But there's three of us, and I think four would be one too many."

"Three ..."

Dick was so focused on the man saying there was a third person and fearing who and where they were that he didn't register the second part about what that would mean for him, at least not until a large shadow fell over him. He looked up to see a big man in a hospital gown, seeing more of him than he wanted to, standing over him.

The big man gripped the poker and pulled it out of the fireplace, the tip glowing orange as embers swirled around it. He walked slowly around to join his companions standing by Dick's feet.

"What the fuck are you doing?" Dick yelled. "I said

you can stay here!"

The man in the security guard uniform smiled. "And I said we're going too." He turned to the big man and told him something with his expression.

Again, Dick was late in processing what was happening, but he didn't have long to worry about it. The big man thrust the poker under his chin, the hot metal searing the flesh as it yielded underneath the pointed tip. The weapon met little resistance as it poked through the floor of its victim's mouth, severing the lingual frenulum and bisecting the tongue. Dick's screams turned to gurgles as blood rushed into his mouth and clogged his throat.

The poker continued its journey through the roof of the man's mouth, singeing and severing his sinuses as it traveled north. Smoke wisped from his nose, and his eyes bulged from their sockets just before the weapon embedded into his brain. Dick had always imagined his last thoughts would be of Ellie. Instead, he found himself watching three demons laugh over him as he died.

CHAPTER 7

Just as Tim finished his declaration that Dick Wilbur would pay for tearing down his treehouse, the power went out. It jarred the boys, and Mikey let out a shocked whimper when everything went dark. They heard another tiny scream, Annie no doubt, from downstairs.

"Shit!" Mikey blurted.

"Quiet down," Tim ordered. "This is the perfect chance to sneak out."

"I don't know..."

"Quit being a pussy. C'mon."

Tim grabbed his friend by the sleeve of his raincoat and pulled him toward the door, carefully pushing it open as he listened to the commotion from the first floor.

"We'll get some candles," he heard Molly say. The quick footsteps that followed told Tim that her mind was already made up, no matter what other instructions she received.

Sure. Perfect excuse to sneak off and suck face with George.

He was about to exit to the hallway when he heard his father's voice shout up to him.

"Tim? You guys okay?"

Tim waited a second before opening the door wider, letting it creak to give the illusion that he wasn't about to sneak out.

"Yeah, Dad! We're good!"

"You got a flashlight up there?"

"Yes, sir!"

"Good. Stay put in your room until the power comes back."

"Sure, Dad. We'll hang up here."

He turned to Mikey and winked even though his friend probably couldn't see it. He tugged his sleeve again, and the boy followed despite his trepidation.

A few minutes later, the duo had managed to sneak down the back stairs and into the kitchen undetected. Tim carefully opened the back door, holding his breath in anticipation that it would squeak like his bedroom door, the same way most of the doors in that old farmhouse did. He let the breath out when it didn't but immediately sucked it back in when the sound of the rain outside intensified without the wood muffling the sound. He grabbed Mikey again and pulled him through, quickly but carefully shutting the door behind him.

Tim crept over to the nearest window and peered

inside, squinting as he observed the darkened interior. He couldn't make out much, but he didn't see his mom or dad rushing into the kitchen with candles or flashlights to investigate. He kept watch for a few more beats before he was confident they were in the clear.

"C'mon. Time to pay Mr. Wilbur a visit."

The rain pounded down on the boys as they crossed over to Dick Wilbur's property. The old man's farmhouse was constructed similarly to the Green homestead, with a long wraparound porch and a stone chimney that was currently belching smoke into the stormy sky. A crack of lightning lit up that sky, followed by a crash of thunder that jarred the boys, even Tim, who was clearly the braver of the two.

"Jesus Christ!" Tim exclaimed.

"I told you this was a bad idea!" Mikey said. "We should just go back."

Tim almost considered it, looking back in the direction of his house. But his resolve returned when he saw the large stump from the tree that had once housed his fortress. He felt his face flush even through the chilly rain. He clenched his fist and told Mikey in no uncertain terms that the plan was still a go. "Fuck that," Tim said as he snatched the shoebox from his friend. "Let's do this."

The boys broke into a run, keeping as wide a berth

from the dwelling as possible to avoid detection. There was a dim, flickering light visible from one window in the front, so they opted to keep to the rear. When they were about ten yards from the back porch, Tim put up his hand to silently signal that they were close enough.

He flipped the lid of the box and grabbed an egg, not hesitating to hurl it at the house. It struck between the back door and the kitchen window, cracking and sending the runny yolk sluicing down the weathered wood.

"Nice one!" Mikey said, trying to sound enthusiastic. "Let's go."

Tim ignored him and grabbed another egg and chucked it. That one splattered on the door frame.

"Hell yeah!" Mikey whispered, sounding even less convincing. "We really should get back."

Again, Tim ignored him, snatching a third egg and rearing his arm back to throw it. He was halfway through his motion when something made him stop abruptly. He lost his grip on the egg, and it fell to the ground through his slick hand, cracking at his feet, the gooey insides splattering his right boot.

The interruption was caused when the back door opened. The boys instinctively froze, caught red-handed in their vandalism.

But it wasn't Dick Wilbur who emerged from the darkened interior of the house. It was a cop. He didn't really look like one. Tim couldn't exactly pinpoint why, but the one thing that stuck out was how his uniform seemed a size too big. But it didn't matter. He was there. And they were screwed.

Oh shit! Tim thought.

"We gotta get out of here," Mikey whispered.

That time, Tim listened to his panicky friend, who was now the one doing the pulling. He turned to run, but as they did, they ran smack into one of the biggest men he had ever seen. The way he was dressed reminded him of Mr. Wilbur, with a flannel shirt and dungarees. But he wasn't Dick Wilbur. Sure, Tim's neighbor was a curmudgeonly old asshole, but the look in this man's eyes was different. They were empty. Soulless.

The big man clamped a large hand on each boy's shoulder. Tim gasped as he felt the meaty fingers dig into his clavicle. When Mikey cried out in pain in front of him, he knew exactly why and how it felt.

The man turned and brought the boys with him, dragging them toward the house. Tim grasped at his wrist and tried to pry it free, but it was too strong. Mikey kicked at his shin and calves, but the impact had no effect as he brought the young teens toward the cop on the porch.

"Tsk, tsk, boys," the cop said. "You should know better than to engage in these types of Mischief Night shenanigans. Vandalism is a serious crime."

"We're sorry!" Mikey said in a panic. "We won't do it again!"

The large man stopped at the threshold but didn't release his captives.

"Oh, I have no doubt about that," the cop agreed. "And if we're being honest, I don't really care. But we can talk about that inside."

He gestured to the big man and stepped aside so he

could pull Tim and Mikey into the house. As soon as they were inside, he shoved them hard, sending them crashing to the floor and eliciting more yelps as they felt the impact of the hard kitchen tile.

Tim hesitated to get up, afraid further movement would cause further pain, but after a few moments, he gathered the courage to push himself up on shaking arms. When he didn't meet resistance, he continued to his feet.

If the man was actually a police officer, the duo was nailed for vandalism. But what if he wasn't? What if he was some kind of pervert? They all heard stories of weirdos taking advantage of kids. Was this something like that? Even if it wasn't, it was clear whatever the men were up to wasn't good. Those were just a few of the million questions that crowded Tim's mind. And none of the potential answers were good for him and Mikey.

He had little time to think about it because the man in the uniform walked over and put his hands on the boys' shoulders. He was gentler than the big man, but Tim's was tender from being squeezed so hard, and he winced despite himself. Mikey did the same.

"Now, boys, I'm going to show you something. I want you to take it in, and then we'll talk about what's next. Understand?"

Tim didn't, but he nodded anyway.

Mikey, in his typical high-strung way, vomited a string of words. "Yes, sir. You got it. Whatever you want us to do. We'll cooperate. Won't we, Tim?"

Tim shot his friend a glare, both telling him to *shut*

the fuck up and to express his anger at revealing his name. He returned the favor. "Sure we will, *Mikey*." He coated his friend's name with as much vitriol as he could muster.

The other boy understood his fuck up and swallowed hard, the gravity of the situation apparent.

The cop ushered them into the living room. In front of the fireplace, which crackled as it spit out embers, providing the only light source in the room, was a recliner. Tim felt icy fingers of fear clasp the back of his neck when he saw a pair of hairy legs sticking out from the other side of the chair. He froze, not wanting to see the rest, but the big man came up behind him and clasped his hand on Tim's neck, doing the same with Mikey. He pushed them around so they could see the grisly sight on the other side. The young teens screamed, dropping any pretense of courage.

Mr. Wilbur way lying on the floor in a large puddle of blood. There was a fire poker impaled through the bottom of his jaw. The dead man's gaping mouth was dark, but Tim knew the poker had made its way through to the top of his neighbor's skull. He knew that because the other end had exited through his cranium. The firelight reflected small white fragments of what had to be bone floating in the plasma that pooled around Mr. Wilbur's head. It reminded Tim of a cracked eggshell. The treehouse incident, which had burned the boy up for weeks, suddenly seemed trivial. The man was a jerk, but he didn't deserve that.

"Do you see, boys?" the cop said as casually as if he was outlining a math problem on a blackboard at school. "Ba'al demands sacrifice, and sacrifice is what we give to him." The man stepped around and crouched in front of them. As scared as Tim was of him, he was grateful the guy blocked the sightline to Mr. Wilbur's body. "Now, normally interlopers would be offered to our Lord as additional tithing. However, your youth intrigues me. I'm sure you've gone to Sunday school and listened to a frumpy old woman drone on about the saints and sacraments, but your minds are still malleable." As if to prove a point, he tapped Tim on the forehead with his index finger. He did the same to Mikey.

"Wha-what does that mean?" Mikey asked, his voice trembling so badly it reminded Tim of the fever he got last year while laid up with the flu. The shivers that had wracked his body had been so intense he felt like his teeth would shatter as they clanked together.

The man turned to Mikey, the slight positional shift of his head giving Tim a fresh view of Wilbur's mangled corpse. He squeezed his eyes shut and put his head down. The quiet bigger man noticed before the cop and reached around to cup the boy's chin, pulling it back upright. Tim looked despite his revulsion, knowing his captor's next move would be to pry his eyes open.

The guy's partner addressed his friend. "It means there's still hope for you. You can learn that salvation lies in service to Ba'al, not a mythical being in the clouds."

"Who's Ba'al?" It was Tim's turn to ask. For a moment, he thought the cop would be pissed, but he actually looked *pleased* at the inquiry.

"Ba'al is our master. He saved me when I was at my lowest, and I repay him by spreading his ministry. He was the god of the Canaanite city, a skilled warrior who rode atop a red horse. When his temple burned, he became the chief secretary of the Underworld, keeper of its public archives. The depth of his knowledge is unsurpassed, knowing all of the past, present, and future. It is this knowledge he blesses me with as I work as his emissary here in the living world."

"What kind of cop are you?" Mikey asked.

Tim could tell he just blurted it out, unable to stop himself, but he felt his abdomen tighten as the question spewed from his buddy's lips.

Again, the man was amused. He looked at the jacket and tugged at it, laughing as he stood up. "Oh, dear child," he said between chuckles. "This is simply a garment. I'm no police officer."

That had been obvious to Tim for some time. Still, hearing the admission only intensified the strangling fear that was constricting his insides. They had to get away somehow or they were fucked.

"What do you want?" Tim asked, trying and failing to sound confident.

"I'm offering you a choice," the man said, all humor snapping out of his demeanor. "Join us in service to Ba'al."

Tim hesitated. He didn't want to answer, afraid to hear the alternative.

But good old Mikey again couldn't help himself. "What's the other choice?"

The man stepped aside, allowing the boys to observe

the husk that was once Dick Wilbur. He didn't say the words, but his eyes conveyed the sentiment. *This is the other choice.*

Tim's brain shut down, and his flight or fight response took control. The big man's hand was still on his left shoulder, so Tim snapped his neck toward him and clamped down hard with his teeth on his captor's hand. The big man wasn't expecting it and growled as he yanked away, the flesh on the back of his hand ripping between Tim's teeth.

Tim knew it wasn't enough, but he was free at that moment, so he whirled and kicked the man in the balls. That staggered him, but Tim's brain clicked on enough to be shocked that it didn't have more of an effect. Just before his mind went back into shutdown, Tim looked toward the kitchen and gave way back to his instincts as he took off running. "Come on, Mikey!" he shouted.

As he reached the back door, a thought came back again, and he felt an absence beside him. He knew he should keep going and worry about it later, but he couldn't help himself. He glanced back just long enough to see Mikey on his stomach, pinned down with the faux cop's foot on his back and the big man's good hand on his ankle. All three regarded Tim.

The men didn't seem too concerned that he was only a few inches from getting away. But it was Mikey's expression that Tim would remember for the rest of his life—the tears that streaked down his cheeks, the intense fear in his eyes. But most of all, Tim would never forget the message they conveyed—the desperate plea that his best friend not abandon him.

Tim's heart broke as he flung the door open and ran back toward his family's property.

CHAPTER 8

George opened the door to the basement and leaned to the left, allowing Molly space to hold out the candle. The small flickering flame did little to illuminate the darkened passage.

George gently took the candle from his girlfriend, his fingertips brushing against the back of her hand as he did.

It wasn't his intention, but the contact sent a chill through parts of Molly's body while simultaneously warming others. *Damn, I'm hard up.*

Molly had been dating George for three months, and they had done little more than make out. She would try to guide his hands to her breasts or down farther south, but he never seemed to catch the hint. She was almost positive he was a virgin.

That wasn't the case with Molly, but as far as her sweet, innocent boyfriend knew, she was pure as the driven snow. He didn't need to know that Brian Carpenter popped her cherry back when she was sixteen. It had nothing to do with their relationship. Neither did her trysts with Rick Baxter, Dwight Rosenthal, Paul Compton, or Rob Zeller. He would probably think that was a lot, but Molly didn't think sleeping with five guys was *that* many.

Oh wait, she forgot Brad Simms. And Craig Collier. But did Craig even count? It was just the tip, and only for a second.

Okay, so six, maybe seven, guys. Was that such a big deal? She knew George would think so. He came from a religious family and had told Molly he was waiting for marriage. That made her want to break his resolve even more. It wasn't that she was trying to *corrupt* him—okay, maybe a little—but she wanted her man to make love to her. Was that so wrong?

Still, it was tricky. George was tall and handsome with muscles a man could only build from years of manual labor. But he also had a sweetness about him, an innocence. And for some reason, Molly found that as attractive as his body. He was so different from any of the jerks she had been with back in high school. He never went past eighth grade, so he wasn't aware of her reputation. She wanted to keep it that way.

It didn't make her any less horny, though.

The young couple had been tasked with retrieving more firewood and candles from the basement. Mom started to object with her usual puritanical reasoning, but Dad, ever practical, shut her down. Kevin Green's tolerance for his wife's recent spiritual journey was high, but in times of crisis, his priority was getting the job done, even if that meant loosening the reins.

Besides, it wasn't like the young couple had time to do anything too scandalous. If they were down in the basement for more than ten or fifteen minutes, it would surely raise her family's suspicions. But that was enough time for Molly to tease George a bit, lay the groundwork to convince him to ditch his celibacy later.

George held out the candle in front of him with one hand while he took Molly's in the other, sending another warm sensation through her.

She leaned into him, intentionally pushing her breasts into his back as she let him lead her down the stairs.

"Where's the firewood?" George asked when they reached the bottom.

Molly kept herself pressed against him as she used her free hand to point to the right side of the spacious basement. A small window provided scant additional light as the raindrops continued to splatter and sluice down the glass from the exterior.

George gently but firmly guided her by the hand in the direction of their task. Oh, the things they could do if he could channel that energy in the bedroom.

Her eyes adjusted to the sparse light, and she was able to make out the shapes of the shelves and cabinets, even if she couldn't discern the finer details.

George's eyes must have acclimated as well, because he picked up his pace as he saw the pile of wood stacked neatly under the window. He put the candle on a small shelf adjacent to the stack and immediately went to work pulling logs off the top and placing them in a smaller pile at his feet, readying them for transport.

Molly seized the opportunity and grabbed his wrist, stopping him from picking up a third log. She used a similarly gentle touch to urge him to turn toward her, pouncing as he did, using her free hand to clasp the back of his neck and pull him in for a kiss.

It wasn't a peck. There was no time for a slow build as her tongue invaded his mouth. She couldn't have seen them even if her own weren't shut, but she knew his eyes must have been as wide as saucers. His shock didn't last long as he returned the kiss, becoming a full participant as their tongues mingled.

After a minute of making out, Molly sensed he was starting to slow, trying to wind down. She wasn't having that yet, so she increased her own pace to compensate for his deficit.

She needed his dick to override his brain, so she added some extra stimuli, grabbing his wrist and guiding it under the front of her crop top and onto her left breast. He resisted, but not so much that she couldn't move his hand where she wanted it. The little brain was winning the battle.

Knowing her boyfriend would not be so bold, Molly reached under her top and nudged George's hand aside just enough to pull the cup of her bra down to allow him unfettered access to her breast. He needed no encouragement to return to groping, his fingers instinctively tweaking her hardened nipple.

Maybe he won't be so hard to convince after all, Molly thought as she moaned into his mouth between kisses.

She knew she was pushing it on time, and her family, Mom especially, would soon get suspicious if they weren't already. But this was the most she had gotten from her beau physically since they started dating. It was worth the risk.

While George continued to work her nipple, his enthusiasm compensating for his lack of skill, Molly made her boldest move yet, breaking away from his lips and moving to his neck, planting slow kisses as he lolled his head back against the firewood that had fallen down his priority list. Knowing he was distracted, she reached down and cupped his crotch through the denim of his overalls. Now it was time for her eyes to bug out. He was huge. She could feel it even through the fabric.

She was more determined than ever to break his willpower.

She stopped kissing his neck and looked him in the eyes, the candle providing enough light to see the lust she brought out of him. Wanting to keep him in that state, she continued to rub him over his clothing as she stared at him.

"You have such a big dick, baby. Don't you wonder what it would feel like inside me?"

"I ...I ...," George stammered, fighting an internal battle between faith and biology.

"I've never had one before," Molly lied, justifying it in her head by thinking, *Well, one that big, at least.* "I'll bet it'd feel so good!"

"Molly, your folks are waiting for us."

Molly stopped rubbing him. He also stopped playing

with her nipple but didn't rush to pull his hand out of her shirt.

"I know, but after we get settled, maybe we just go for it?"

"Go for it?" George asked, his naivety starting to kill her mood.

"You know... FUCK!" That last word was the one she intended to use. She meant to use it to describe what she wanted to do with her boyfriend. Instead, the expletive came out as a declaration of shock. She jumped back, George's hand slipping out from under her top in the process.

"What is it?" her boyfriend asked, hurriedly attempting to adjust himself to hide his erection.

Molly trembled, no longer with desire but with terror, as she pointed toward the window. When George turned to look, he saw exactly what had scared his girlfriend.

A skinny man crouched outside the small windows, leering at the couple. He was wearing a white leisure suit that reminded Molly of the one John Travolta wore in *Saturday Night Fever*. His gaunt face was slicked by the rain, and stringy tangles of dark hair matted his forehead. The man's expression was obscene, but the most disturbing thing was his pants. They were still on, but his belt was unfastened and his fly was down, the flaps hanging open on either side. He looked to be bracing himself against the house with one arm that extended past the window frame. The other hand was embedded in his pants, rubbing furiously.

"What the heck?" George yelled, his innocence

shining through even in a moment of fear.

The man momentarily looked disappointed as the couple ceased their foreplay and focused on him. But something about their reaction tickled him. He smiled widely and licked his lips obscenely before casually standing and sauntering out of view.

Molly bolted toward the stairs, and George followed, stopping only long enough to grab the candle. He didn't bother with the wood, nearly tripping over the small pile as he scrambled to catch up with her.

A flashlight beam cut through the darkness in the doorway at the top of the stairs. Molly felt relief when her father's voice followed. "Molly? Are you okay?"

Molly took the stairs two at a time and threw her arms around him, tears starting immediately, shifting from a sexed up eighteen-year-old back to a girl who needed nothing more than for her daddy to protect her.

Kevin squeezed her as George lumbered up the stairs behind her. His breath was rapid and shallow. He was in too good of shape to be winded, so Molly assumed he was plain scared shitless.

Mom had joined them, along with Aunt Susan. Molly didn't see Franky or Annie, but she assumed the moms told them to hang back while they investigated.

Tim and Mikey were probably upstairs, oblivious to their surroundings as usual. The real question was where was the man who had been watching them?

"What's going on?" Mom asked, sounding more angry than concerned. "Did he try to get inappropriate with you?"

"No!" Molly shouted emphatically, knowing damn

well she was the one driving any impropriety, not that she would admit that. Even at that moment.

"No ma'am," George concurred. "We was just, uh, gathering firewood when we saw a fella staring in at us from the window!"

Despite the circumstances, Molly was impressed George had it in him to lie to her mom about what they were doing. He must have assumed—correctly—that the truth would get him in bigger trouble. Still, his stuttering made the lie less than convincing. Thankfully, her parents focused on the real problem.

"Who?" Dad asked. "Did you recognize him?"

"No, sir, Mr. Green. He was skinny and wearing a fancy white suit. Like that Travolta guy. And he was, um ..."

"What, boy? Spit it out."

"He was diddling his wiener, sir."

"Jesus Christ!" Kevin shouted, and extricated himself from his daughter's grip. Her mom reached out to offer her own arms for comfort, but she hugged George instead as her father stormed into the living room.

Kevin burst through the front door, holding the twelve-gauge shotgun out in front of him, his flashlight pressed against the barrel in an attempt to see through the rain. He didn't step off the covered porch, trying to keep his weapon dry. He scanned the area in front of him and didn't see anyone. Being as quiet as he could, he moved to one end of the porch, leaning around the corner to inspect the side. It was clear as far as he could tell, so he repeated the sweep on the other side, again finding nothing.

Frustrated, he returned to the front door. He was ready to go back into the house when something to the right caught his eye. He moved toward that section of the porch and shined the light on his pickup truck. The passenger side was visible from his vantage point, and he saw both tires were flat. He leaned out and trained the beam on Susan's car parked behind his, and saw her passenger side tires were flat too. No way that was a coincidence. Someone had slashed them.

He kept his gun focused on the front of the property and backed in through the front door, shutting it behind him and locking it before pulling the chain across for additional security.

The family had moved into the living room. They had gathered a few more candles, enough for the patriarch to see the fearful looks on their faces. Molly was huddled against George, who was standing just off the threshold of the kitchen. Debra and Susan bookended the two youngest children on the couch. For the moment, they seemed more confused than scared.

"What's happening?" Debra asked.

"Did you see him?" Molly added before he could answer.

"There was no one there," Kevin said as he moved over to the window, drawing the curtains closed. He repeated the action on the next one, nodding to George.

That signal he picked up, and he let Molly go and started pulling the curtains closed on his side of the room. Molly helped close the last one.

Susan got off the couch and approached her brother, getting close enough that he could see the look in her eye.

"You saw something," she whispered, a statement, not a question. That followed when Kevin didn't answer. "What?"

Kevin looked over her shoulder at the rest of his family before turning his attention back to his sister. "The cars—the tires are flat."

"Oh my god," Susan said, putting a hand over her mouth too late to stifle the words. "What do we do?"

Before Kevin could respond, a thought entered his mind, followed by a wave of panic. In all the commotion, he hadn't noticed someone was missing. He ran to the stairs and shouted up. "Tim!"

He didn't wait for the answer that didn't come before bounding up the stairs and rushing to Tim's room. He flung the door open and immediately confirmed his fear. Tim was gone. His friend too. Kevin didn't think about it for too long. He ran back downstairs.

Debra was standing at the foot of the stairs, waiting. "Where's Tim?" she asked.

"Gone," Kevin said matter-of-factly as he grabbed a raincoat off the hook. He would have to do his best to keep the shotgun dry. He knew his wife had other questions, but he turned his focus to George. "You know how to use a gun, George?"

"Yes, sir," George said.

Kevin didn't follow up as he unlocked a cabinet in the corner of the room, grabbing a Browning BAR-22 hunting rifle and handing it to George, along with a box of bullets.

"You can handle this one?"

"Yes, sir, Mr. Green."

"Good. Now, once I go outside, you lock that door behind me."

"Kev-" Susan said, as Debra remained silent, chewing her cuticles.

Kevin didn't acknowledge his sister as he continued his instructions to George. "When I come back, I'll knock twice, then three more times. You understand?"

"Yes, sir."

"Repeat it."

"You'll knock twice, then three times, when you get back."

"Good," Kevin said, patting the boy's shoulder. "Anyone but me, my son, or his friend tries to get in here, you shoot. No hesitation. Got me?"

There was no *yes, sir* that time, just a nervous nod.

"Ok," he said, turning back to Susan and Debra. "I'm going to go find our son."

CHAPTER 9

The rain was finally slowing as Kevin left the house to look for Tim. While he didn't know for sure, he thought his best option was to make his way to Dick Wilbur's house. His son didn't take too kindly to their new neighbor forcing the Greens to tear down their boy's beloved treehouse. He also knew his son wasn't one to let things go. He had gotten into more than a couple of fights at school over various slights, whether real or perceived. Combine that with the opportunity this faux holiday presented, and it was a good bet that Tim and Mikey were out committing acts of mischief against their nemesis.

Dumb kids.

Kevin was careful to keep his eyes on his periphery as he made his way to the tree line. Once past the first row of white oaks, he broke into a sprint, afraid time was not on his side to reach his son before the intruders on his land did.

He was halfway to Wilbur's property when he heard footsteps rapidly approaching in front of him. The leaves were soaked and devoid of their normal dry crunch, but whoever was coming toward him was moving haphazardly, unconcerned with stealth.

Kevin dropped to a crouch and aimed his gun in the direction of the footfalls. Visibility was limited, and he tensed, knowing it may be Tim or Mikey coming toward him, or even Dick Wilbur, despite Wilbur's personal animosity toward his neighbor. He couldn't just shoot first and ask questions later. He only hoped that if whoever emerged was hostile he had enough time to identify him and take him down before it was too late.

"Stop right there!" Kevin ordered as the unknown party drew closer. The footsteps stopped abruptly, and after a few very long moments, Tim's voice responded.

"Dad! It's me!"

Kevin immediately righted himself and pointed the gun at the ground as he ran toward his son's voice. Even through the rain, he could hear the distress in it. The father and son closed ground, and Tim barreled into his dad, throwing his arms around him. Kevin allowed the boy a moment to take in the comfort of his embrace but broke it and pushed him back gently to examine him.

"Are you hurt?" Kevin asked as he looked his son over. He appeared physically okay, but his bloodshot eyes betrayed his panic. "What happened?"

"We went to Mr. Wilbur's," Tim explained, the words spewing from his mouth without pause between sentences. "We were going to egg his house because of what he did, that's all, I swear, but there were two other guys there. One of them was dressed like a cop or something, but he wasn't, he was crazy, and there was this really big guy who didn't talk who grabbed us. Then they brought us in, and Mr. Wilbur was dead, but I got away. But they still have Mikey." He finally paused and swallowed hard before adding, "We have to help him, Dad. I think they're going to kill him."

Kevin considered his next move while taking in the desperation in Tim's eyes. He thought about sending his son back home but didn't know if the man who peeped at Molly was one of the intruders Tim had described. Whoever it was may still be stalking their house, and if he sent Tim back, that could put him in direct peril. It was better to keep the boy by his side.

"Tim, listen to me carefully," Kevin said. "We're going to go to Mr. Wilbur's house to get Mikey." He saw his son tense, but he didn't protest. "Were these men you saw armed? Did they have guns?"

Tim shook his head. "I didn't see any guns. They killed Mr. Wilbur with a fire poker, but they weren't carrying anything I saw."

Kevin nodded while maintaining eye contact. "Okay. Well, I have a gun. I can't send you back because I don't know if anyone else is out there. So, you're going to stay close to me, and I'm going to keep you safe. Understand?"

The boy nodded back, and Kevin grabbed him by the hand and led him toward Dick Wilbur's farm.

Tim screamed as they emerged from the woods and onto their neighbor's property. Kevin saw it a second later, and he didn't blame his son one bit for his reaction. The sight in front of them was horrid.

Mikey was sprawled out over the stump where the tree that once was home to Tim's tree house had stood. Kevin didn't need to get closer to know the boy was dead. His arms and legs hung limply over the edges of what remained of the tree, and his shirt was cut down the middle, the fabric hanging loosely on either side. Underneath, he was sliced stomach to sternum, and ropes of bloody intestines draped over his corpse. There were multiple marks that looked to be carved into the teen's face, although Kevin couldn't say what the strange symbols were. It looked cult-like.

Kevin didn't hesitate to turn Tim to him, hugging the boy tightly with one arm while keeping the gun aimed in front of him. His son sobbed into his chest, devastated at the grim discovery.

"I'm sorry I left him, Dad. This is my fault. I was scared. I was so scared. He's dead because of me."

"No, son," Kevin said. "If you stayed, they would have killed you too. You did the right thing. You tried to get help." That only made Tim cry harder. Kevin tightened his grip, trying to stabilize the boy's trembling body. "Listen to me. We can't do anything for him now. We have to get back to our house and wait for the police."

He didn't mention to Tim that they didn't have any way of actually calling the police, but that didn't matter. They needed to get to the sanctuary of their own home. He and George both had long guns, and the women could probably handle the pistols from his collection. They had no other choice but to arm themselves and wait this nightmare out.

"We have to move now, Tim. Can you do that?"

The boy broke away, not daring to turn around and see what was left of his best friend. He looked up at his father to nod his acknowledgement, but Kevin saw his eyes bug out. "Dad!" was all Tim could get out before Kevin felt something smack him in the back of the head. It felt like a bowling ball, but in actuality, it was the giant fist of Wallace Little. He stumbled forward, knocking his son over as he fell. He also lost his shotgun as the impact, combined with the slick wood-grain stock, made it impossible to hold on to. The gun and flashlight landed a few feet in front of him.

He rolled to his side to allow Tim to get up, but he felt his body lift off the ground before being unceremoniously tossed back, farther away from his weapon. As he landed on his back, his wind left him and his mouth filled with water as he struggled to draw back the air he had lost.

A large shape filled his blurred vision. As it cleared, he saw a big man in overalls standing over him. The sleeves of the flannel shirt underneath were rolled up, and the rain washed fresh blood from his forearms. He reached down and grabbed Kevin by his shirt, pulling him to a standing position.

Kevin regained enough of his faculties to hit the man in the mouth with a right cross. The assailant's head snapped to the side when the blow landed, but he slowly turned back to Kevin with a sick smile spread across his face. The punch split the man's upper lip, and blood stained his teeth as it dripped down his chin. Even though it did damage, it wasn't going to stop him.

The man returned the favor by slamming his forehead into the bridge of Kevin's nose. Kevin saw a flash of blinding white light followed by stars circling his vision as he crashed back to the ground. His eyes watered as he rolled onto his stomach. He searched for Tim, who was standing several yards back, toward the tree line, frozen in horror as he watched his father get beaten.

"Tim," Kevin said, his voice hoarse and cracked. "Tim!" he yelled again, that one louder, more forceful. "Run!"

For the second time that night, Tim ran away, leaving someone he loved at the mercy of the maniacs.

CHAPTER 10

Susan stood off to the side of the window, pulling the curtain aside just enough so she could see the front of the house. The rain had slowed but still hampered visibility. She could see some of the driveway, but not so far that she could observe the road.

Behind her, Franky and Annie were playing with their toys on the floor, using a candle to illuminate whatever interaction they had concocted between her son's army men and her niece's Raggedy Ann doll. She was thankful the two youngest seemed to be taking the craziness in stride.

Molly and George sat on the couch. Molly had her arm hooked around her boyfriend's. The young man held the rifle in his lap with shaky hands as his knee bounced up and down like a jackhammer. His physique was solid and made him look intimidating at first glance, but it was obvious he didn't have the stomach for this type of conflict.

Debra remained seated at the table where she had been when Susan first arrived. Her sister-in-law was quiet, with her hands folded atop a pile of those pamphlets. Her eyes were closed, and her mouth moved wordlessly. She was praying. Susan didn't share the woman's piety but couldn't fault her. With her son and husband outside with a potential stalker, divine intervention may be necessary.

Kevin had been gone for twenty minutes. She didn't know how far Dick Wilbur's farm was, but it couldn't be that far. *Come on, Kev*, she thought. *Where the hell are you?*

Maybe it was some form of divine intervention, because the moment she finished her thought, a figure emerged from the woods off to the left of the driveway, only it was too small to be her brother. It was Tim.

The boy ran as if he was being chased by the devil himself. His arms flailed in his uncontrolled sprint. As he got closer to the house, Susan didn't see anyone come out of the woods after him. Where was Kevin?

Tim was almost on the porch when Susan sprang to action. She let the curtain fall and hurried to the door, working quickly to unlock it.

Molly and George hopped from the couch. George fumbled with the rifle as he struggled to take a defensive posture, while Molly posed the question in a shaky voice. "Aunt Suse? What are you doing?"

Susan answered by flinging the door open, allowing her nephew to stumble through. The boy clearly thought he was going to slam into the door because its absence screwed up his momentum, causing him to fall to the floor, barely bracing himself with his hands to keep from smacking his face into the wood.

As soon as he cleared the door, Susan shut and relocked it. Tim scrambled off the floor and rushed to Debra, who had risen from her chair and rushed over to embrace her son.

Susan kept her eye on him as she moved to Franky and put a reassuring hand on his shoulder now that his attention was diverted from his play to the scene before him.

"Where's your father?" Susan asked before Debra could.

The boy extracted himself from his mother's grip, and his head swung as if on a swivel from his mother to his aunt to his sisters and cousin as he spewed a panicked explanation. "Dad's in trouble! There were guys at Mr. Wilbur's farm! They killed Mr. Wilbur, and...and...they killed Mikey too!" His voice cracked and softened as he delivered the news of his best friend's demise. Still, he didn't have time to dwell on it because he knew his father was in grave danger. "The big man attacked Dad! He needs our help!"

That was all Susan needed to hear. She had left Woodbury and come to her brother's home to escape a monster, one who had tormented her for years. Now she found herself in the path of different, even deadlier monsters. Her brother and her family were in that path too. Her son was in that path. Something woke up inside her. Years of abuse and fear had threatened to crush her if she let it. She vowed it wouldn't when she left her husband, and she refused to let it at that moment, when her brother needed her.

She only had to spare a glance in George's direction to know he wouldn't be much help. At least the boy had the good sense to keep his finger off the trigger. The way it was twitching, he may very well have shot somebody in the room.

Debra pulled Tim back in for another hug but offered no suggestions on how to help Kevin. She simply held her sobbing son.

Molly's eyes darted back and forth between the older women, also lacking faith in her docile boyfriend to help her father.

Susan acted without further deliberation. "George, give me the rifle," she ordered, approaching him with her arms out.

"But Mr. Green told me ..." he protested, trailing off before finishing his sentence.

Susan took the rifle. George didn't necessarily hand it over willingly, but he didn't object, either. He just stood slack jawed as she took charge.

Susan knew her way around a gun. She and Kevin had grown up on a farm not much different than the one her brother now owned. Their dad made sure both of them knew how to shoot. Charles was also insistent that she understood firearm safety and care, or at least he did back when he still presented himself as a loving husband and father.

"What are you doing, Susan?" Debra asked as her sister-in-law checked to confirm the gun was loaded properly.

"I'm going to help Kevin."

Everyone's reaction to the declaration was different.

"George?" Molly asked, looking at her boyfriend with disappointment.

"I, maybe I should go, Ms. Green."

"No," she said. She believed he was sincere and likely would have fought his fear to try to help her brother. But she wasn't confident he would pull the trigger if he needed to. Hell, would she? She had taken near-endless abuse for years. Just because she found the resolve only a few hours ago to flee that situation, was she somehow suddenly equipped for a showdown with psychotic murderers? "You stay here and look after everyone," she continued before addressing Debra. "Do you know where Kevin keeps his other guns?"

"Yes, but-"

Susan didn't give her the chance to finish. It felt like her sister-in-law lacked urgency, and she couldn't understand why. It was bordering on pissing her off. She continued her instructions, ignoring the word but.

"Get George one. Molly, have you shot a gun before?"

"Yes," her niece answered.

Again, Susan gave a directive to Debra. "Get one for you and Molly too. George, keep your eye on the window and don't let anyone in that isn't me or Kevin. Like he told you, shoot them if there's any doubt."

"Susan, I really don't think—"

Again, Debra didn't get to finish as Susan crouched to address Franky and Annie.

"Listen, I want you to go play your game in the closet. It'll be more fun in there, like your own little fort."

The children were skeptical. Maybe they didn't fully grasp what was going on, but they still knew something wasn't right.

"Where are you going, Mommy?" Franky asked.

"I have to go help Uncle Kevin," she answered.

"But what about the bad men out there? The ones who hurt Tim's friend?"

Damn it. Of course they heard. They weren't toddlers. They were more than capable of knowing something was wrong.

"George is a big guy. If anyone tries to get in here that isn't supposed to be, he'll take them down, no problem. Isn't that right, George?" She shot him a look that was as encouraging as much as it was threatening. It said, *I'm putting my faith in you, so don't fuck this up.*

George swallowed hard but was able to get out an acceptable, "Yes, ma'am."

"See? George and Aunt Debra and Cousin Molly will take care of you. Okay?" Franky and Annie nodded in unison, and Susan added a firm but gentle, "Now do as I say."

The kids got up and headed to the closet. To Susan's surprise, Tim let go of his mother, wiped his eyes, and told the young ones, "I'll come play with you." She didn't know if the thirteen-year-old wanted to hide himself or if that was his way of doing his part, but either way, she was grateful.

Watching as the trio slipped into the spacious closet, Susan retrieved her raincoat and hurriedly donned it. She looked toward Debra, expecting protest while seeking concurrence. She received neither. If they survived this, she would ask Kevin just what the hell was going on with his wife, but *survival* was the key word at the moment.

"Debra," she asked, "How far is your neighbor's house?"

"About a quarter-mile east."

"I'll be back," Susan said.

She exited the house, and immediately, a cold gust of wind hit her in the face. The rain wasn't as heavy as when she arrived, but it was still falling steadily. As she stepped off the porch and onto the wet grass, the shrill, high-pitched howl of a coyote emanated from the woods—another predator in a world that felt full of them.

But with Kevin's life on the line, Susan couldn't let that deter her. She started toward Dick Wilbur's farm.

CHAPTER 11

Molly was as pissed as she was scared. She couldn't even look at George. Her boyfriend's adorable innocence was cute when she was trying to seduce him, but the oaf failing to man up in their dangerous situation drained all the attraction she felt toward him. She almost wanted to kick his ass out, but despite his reticence to take charge and act, he was still the most physically imposing presence in the house by far.

Hopefully the mere sight of him would be enough to deter any intruders. Because if he ended up opening his big, dumb mouth, they were fucked.

"Are you okay, Molly?" George asked, picking up on her energy.

"I can't believe you made my aunt go out there by herself!"

"She told me to stay here."

"Ugh!" Molly blurted, throwing her hands up in

exasperation. "If what Tim said is true, there are literal murdering psychopaths attacking my dad!" Her anger melded with grief, knowing there was a good chance her father was dead. Her next words were shaky. "If he dies, it's your fault!"

George was clearly feeling guilty. He looked as if he would crash through the floor from the weight of it. Molly didn't feel bad for him. Not with what was at stake.

George reached out and put his arm on her shoulder. "Molly ...," he said, trailing off without saying anything else.

She pulled away from him as if his hand was on fire, giving him one more disapproving glare before stomping over to the couch and plopping down with her arms crossed.

"George."

Molly heard her mother address her soon-to-be-ex boyfriend. The calmness in her voice was unsettling. She was so tunnel-visioned in her anger at George she hadn't considered that her mother was eerily calm considering the danger they were in.

Then again, Mom usually kept a cool head about her in times of crisis, like when Tim fell out of his treehouse and broke his arm. Molly remembered her being so calm, while her brother, ten at the time, screamed bloody murder.

In fact, it felt like the only time Debra got worked up was when Molly engaged in behavior her mother deemed *immoral*. Annie choking on a potato chip? Mom will do the Heimlich and go back about her business. Molly's skirt is too short? Hell to pay. Still, they had never experienced anything like this, and her mother's reaction—or lack thereof—didn't feel right.

"Yes, ma'am?" George asked, having no such concern.

"My husband keeps his pistols locked up in a safe in the basement. Be a dear and come help me with them. Grab a candle."

He did as instructed.

Molly asked, "Want me to come too?"

"No, sweetie," Debra said. "Stay here in case the younger kids come out. They'll be frightened if they're here alone."

How about me? she thought. *I'm pretty fucking frightened too!* Molly knew better than to articulate the thought, however, especially punctuated with profanity, so she simply offered a weak, "Okay."

If she was furious with George before, she was damn near apoplectic now. She had no delusions that she was some kind of protector. She knew she couldn't fight multiple grown men if they tried to break in.

George looked at her apologetically as he went to follow Debra, who had already made her way to the kitchen.

Molly whispered to him through gritted teeth. "Hurry the fuck up."

"We'll only be a minute," he replied, trying to sound reassuring even though he had no clue how long it would take to gather the guns.

A moment later, George was gone, and she was alone in the living room with the fireplace as the only light source. She felt cold and borderline nauseous, fear permeating every corner of her mind, manifesting adverse physical effects. Other than the soft crackle of the fire, the room was quiet. Too quiet.

Molly suddenly realized she couldn't hear her siblings and cousin in the closet. She dug her fingers into the couch cushions, nearly ripping the well-worn fabric. Leaning her head back, she listened carefully for any sound coming from the hiding spot. Nothing.

Intrusive thoughts shoved their way into her brain. She pictured the creep hiding in the closet, just waiting for the right time to strike. Two eight-year-olds and a boy who was barely a teenager himself would be the perfect opportunity.

As much as she didn't want to, she had to check.

She forced herself to get off the couch, moving slowly to avoid making too much noise, splitting her focus between silent motions and keeping her ears alert for any noise from the closet. Molly felt particularly helpless without a weapon. Fortunately, she saw a solution out of the corner of her eye.

Keeping quiet as she took the detour, she crept to the fireplace and carefully removed a poker from the tool stand. Despite her best effort, the metal squeaked against the holder as she withdrew it. She held her breath as she listened for a reaction, but none came.

Regaining her confidence to proceed, she exhaled and tiptoed to the closet. She still heard nothing from within. Before she opened the door, ready to face whatever or whoever may be inside, she pressed her ear to the wood, trying to hear.

There was still nothing, so she reached for the knob. The brass felt cold to the touch as she wrapped her fingers around it. Her heart quickened as she started to turn it while tightening her grip on the poker in her opposite hand. Just as she was about to commit, however, she heard a whisper from the other side.

"Those army men are really cool." It was Tim's voice.

Franky followed. "Thanks. I like to pretend I'm this one."

"Totally cool," Tim replied

"My doll is cool too," Annie chimed in.

"Of course she is!" Tim said, showing kindness to his little sister.

Molly exhaled in relief and carefully released the doorknob. She thought about tapping on the door and asking if they were okay, but that felt like a dumb question. Of course they weren't okay. They were, however, keeping it together and doing as they were told, and that was enough. Checking in may only have disrupted things.

As she stepped back from the closet, ready to return to her seat, she heard a heavy thud from the kitchen, like something very large hit the floor.

"Mom?" she called, whispering as loud as she could while still being able to classify it as a whisper. Her mother didn't answer, so she called to her boyfriend, forgetting to regulate her voice. "George?" He didn't answer either. Molly looked toward the kitchen. The framing of the entryway was visible thanks to the firelight, but the room beyond was a dark void.

Molly gripped the poker tightly and took a tentative step forward, calling out again. "Mom? George?" She prayed for a reply to absolve her of having to enter the darkened room. "Are you okay?"

Again, there was no answer. She was going to have to check on them. As silently as she had approached the closet, she made her way to the kitchen. Despite the chill seeping its way into the powerless house, her palms were slick with sweat. She was afraid she would drop the poker, so she wiped her free hand on her pants before transferring the weapon and repeating the process on the empty one. Able to maintain a better grip, she swapped the poker back to her dominant hand.

Her breathing intensified, and the rapid inhalations followed by stunted exhalations rang in her ears. The sounds seemed impossibly loud, even feeling like it was drowning out her carefully calibrated footfalls.

As she got closer, her eyes adjusted the same way they had in the basement earlier, familiarity aiding her vision as the shapes of the kitchen fixtures took form. Stepping into the darkened room, Molly saw a small light source off to the side. It was one of the candles, resting on the counter by the back door. The tiny glow didn't add a lot of illumination, but it was better than nothing. She moved to retrieve it but stopped suddenly when her right foot, clad only in a thin sock, came down on something wet.

Molly gasped at the sensation but stopped herself from crying out. She really didn't want to see what the substance was but felt compelled to find out. She eschewed caution and hurried to grab the candle, her left foot also becoming soggy from the unidentified puddle. When she grabbed the light source, she didn't hesitate to inspect her feet.

Another gasp escaped as she saw her red socks, which had been white when she put them on. Yet another gasp caught in her throat when she saw the wetness was a pool of fresh blood. It smeared the tile and filled the grout lines. There was *so much* of it!

The terrified teen whimpered as she held out the candle, following the crimson path to its source, which didn't take long to discover. She braced herself on the counter, crouching as she extended the hand with the candle, trying to see as far in front of her as she could without having to move forward, petrified of finding out whose blood it was.

A second later, she found out.

The candlelight fell on George's dead eyes. They were missing the spark of life but also looked normal, like he had been taken by surprise and died before he even realized he was in danger. Molly wasn't even conscious of her own motion as she moved the light to inspect her dead boyfriend's body.

A meat cleaver was embedded deep in the boy's throat. From the look of it, the blade had made it halfway in. Either the killer was that strong or the cleaver was that sharp.

Molly dropped the candle. It fell sideways into the pool of George's blood, the flame extinguishing with a muted sizzle. She brought her now-empty hand up to her mouth to stifle her scream. She didn't need to as she felt another hand clamp over it.

"Shhh," Debra said behind her. "Don't scream."

While terrified, Molly released some tension knowing it was her mother. She slowly nodded as the older woman withdrew her hand. Molly swallowed hard before asking the question. "Who did this?"

"It was Ba'al's command," Debra said robotically. "He wanted a sacrifice."

"Who?" Molly asked in panicked confusion. "A sacrifice? George?" She got an unexpected answer as her mother brought a butcher knife to the center of her jugular.

Debra whispered in a voice that, while it sounded like her, felt different. "He's not the sacrifice."

CHAPTER 12

The true horror of the situation revealed itself to Susan when she saw Mikey's mutilated body draped over the tree stump. Until that moment, there had been hope that the night wasn't actually a matter of life or death. There was a storm and a power outage, yes, as well as the Peeping Tom, but maybe Molly had just seen their neighbor stopping by to check on them. Or perhaps it was a stranded motorist looking for help?

Then there were the slashed tires. It was Mischief Night, after all. It could easily have been a prank. A fucked-up prank for sure, but it may not have been more than that.

And maybe Mikey hadn't been killed. Tim could have been telling a wild story to cover up a failed attempt to vandalize Dick Wilbur's house. Why he would say his friend was killed Susan didn't know, but there remained the possibility that wasn't what happened.

But when Susan cleared the trees and emerged onto the Wilbur farm, she saw the decimated body of a boy only a few years older than her son and knew the danger was all too real. Fortunately, she didn't have time to dwell on the grisly scene. Her attention was diverted by a commotion to her left. She followed the sound and saw a large man straddling someone lying on their back. The guy on top, wearing overalls and a flannel shirt, was raining heavy blows on his opponent. From her vantage point, she could see the victim was alive.

Their feet thrashed under the attacker as they tried to defend themself. Was it Kevin?

"Hey!" Susan yelled as she rushed toward the fracas. "Get off of him!"

The man either didn't hear or didn't care, because he continued the assault. The recipient of the beating continued to struggle, but their efforts appeared to diminish, the thrashing becoming less emphatic.

Susan rushed forward, screaming again. "Fucking stop!" Still the attack continued. The rain had slowed to a drizzle, so assuming the man wasn't hearing impaired, he should have been able to hear her. Perhaps he did but didn't consider her a threat.

She aimed the rifle toward the sky. Even though the storm had let up, the weapon was wet. She knew her brother kept his guns in good working order, and raindrops were a different story than being fully submerged, but she still prayed it wouldn't jam.

The prayer was answered when she pulled the

trigger and the crack of the gunshot echoed across the field.

The gun's report was enough to draw the man's attention, but it didn't appear to concern him. He stopped punching and pushed up on his knees, continuing to hover over his victim, whose legs twitched twice in rapid succession before falling limp.

Oh my God, are they dead? Susan thought as she watched the big man rise to his feet. He didn't hurry to turn around despite knowing there was a gun likely aimed in his direction. Susan watched as he lowered and tilted his head like he was trying to ascertain if the person beneath him was still breathing, the person who she could now clearly see was her brother.

"Kevin!" she cried. *That* earned her the man's attention.

He slowly pivoted to face her. He was indeed massive. Yes, he was tall, but it was the sheer mass of his physique that stood out. He looked like one of those Mr. Olympia bodybuilders. His meat-hook-sized fists were balled at his sides, and Susan could see the blood, diluted by the rain, trickling across his knuckles as it dripped to the ground below. A sinister smile spread across the man's face, and his dark eyes gleamed with malevolent delight as he eyed Susan.

She aimed the rifle and did everything she could to keep the shakiness from her voice as she commanded, "Don't fucking move!"

The man ignored her and took a step in her direction. That was enough. Susan knew threats wouldn't work. She had tried them repeatedly with Charles, threatening to leave him and take Franky. She even threatened to go to Freeman, to report him to the very department he worked for. Each time, he called her bluff, and she caught a beating for it. She knew there were no words that would compel this man to stop, so she acted and pulled the trigger, denying him another step.

The second gunshot seemed louder than the first. The bullet struck home a second before the man brought his hand to his forehead, at the point of impact. He didn't have time to inspect the wound as he pitched backward and toppled to the ground like a felled tree, landing next to Kevin.

Susan continued to act decisively, rushing to her downed sibling while keeping the smoking barrel trained on the man next to him. When she saw the state of her brother, she pulled in an intake of breath so sharp it felt as if it constricted her heart, sending a hot wave of pain across her chest.

The left side of Kevin's face had taken the worst of it. Large red and purple blotches blanketed half his visage. His eye on that side was swollen completely shut, reminding her of Sylvester Stallone in that boxing movie Charles loved so damn much. Her brother's lip was twice its normal size and split in multiple spots, seeping blood over his misaligned jaw.

He wasn't moving, and Susan couldn't tell if he was breathing. Fear strangled her upon the realization that he might be dead. It took her almost five minutes to cover the distance between properties. Add that to the time it took Tim to get back and the few minutes of deliberation, Kevin had been under attack by that monster for close to fifteen minutes. The man was clearly toying with his victim, taking sadistic pleasure at inflicting as much pain as possible to the point where the inevitable killing blow would be an act of mercy.

"Kev," she whispered as she reached to stroke his cheek. She moved tentatively, hesitating to make contact with his battered skin, as if the slightest touch would shatter him like a fragile crystal ornament.

As soon as her fingertips grazed his swollen face, Kevin's eyes shot open and he exhaled sharply as if he had been holding his breath until the moment his lungs coerced the air out. The sudden exhalation was too forceful and caused him to cough, expelling a wad of bloody sputum that sprayed upward like a fountain before falling back on his chin with a splat. A second cough produced more. That time, the gob landed in his mouth and slid down his throat, causing him to choke. He was too disoriented to protect himself, so Susan rolled him on his side, allowing him to clear the gunk from his esophagus.

"Kev!" she shouted while slapping his back to aid him in clearing his windpipe. "Can you get up? We have to get back!"

His sister's voice helped bridge the gap back to lucidity. He struggled to his knees and asked a one-word question. "Tim?"

"He's okay," Susan said. "He's back at the house with Debra and the kids."

That motivated him to move, and with Susan's help, he struggled to his feet, surveying the area as he did. The big man was down and motionless, with blood pooling around the left side of his head. But it wasn't him Kevin was looking for. He saw his shotgun close to the downed psycho and lunged to grab it, nearly falling over in the process. Susan held on to him and keep him upright as he retrieved the weapon. Unfortunately, the flashlight next to it was off, the bulb having shattered when it fell. She was lucky to have made it there without one, but at least Kevin was here now to help them find their way in the dark

Positioning himself upright so he could lean on his sister, Kevin cleared his throat and spat another wad of blood-streaked phlegm before declaring, "Let's go."

CHAPTER 13

Tim was watching his sister and cousin play quietly in the candlelight when he heard the knock at the closet door. All three of them fell still, unsure how to respond. They hadn't worked out any type of signal or specific knock to let them know it was safe to come out. Annie and Franky looked at Tim, who put his finger to his lips, silently instructing them to keep quiet, knowing that whoever was on the other side of that door—hopefully his mom or older sister—would have to announce themselves before the three of them came out.

It felt like forever, waiting for a reply. Tim could see the younger kids' expressions turn increasingly anxious as each moment passed. Two more knocks echoed through the small space, and Tim did everything he could to not jump. That time, however, a gentle and familiar woman's voice followed—his mom's.

"Tim," Debra whispered from the other side of the door. "It's okay. You can come out now."

Annie and Franky looked relieved but still didn't act, allowing the older boy to respond on their behalf.

"Are you sure?" Tim asked. As soon as the question left his lips, he realized he wasn't sure why he asked it. It was no doubt his mother's voice, and it didn't sound any different than usual. But still, something gave him pause. Maybe it was because Aunt Susan was the one who told them to stay in the closet. He knew his mother's authority superseded his aunt's, but something about the way Susan took charge made Tim hesitate, wondering if she would approve of them leaving the hiding spot. After all, he was responsible for her son too.

"Tim?" his mother asked again, her voice a little louder.

Tim waited a beat then finally answered. "Coming," he said while turning his palms out and patting the air in front of him, gesturing for the younger children to stay where they were. Neither acknowledged him, but they didn't move, either.

Tim took his time getting to his feet and maneuvering around Annie and Franky to the front of the closet. He took a deep breath as he twisted the knob and pushed the door open, revealing the dimly lit living room on the other side. He didn't see his mother.

"Mom?" he called, remaining on the interior side of the closet, keeping his hand on the doorknob, unconsciously tightening his grip. Seconds passed without a response. Just as Tim was ready to shut the door again, he heard his mother's voice from over by the front door.

"It's okay, Tim," Mom said. "You can come out."

Tim poked his head around the corner and could see the shape of his mother's form over by the window to the right of the front door. The rain had picked back up, and heavy raindrops battered the pane, punctuating the constant crackle from the fireplace.

"Mom?" Tim asked again, taking a step out of the closet.

"It's okay, Timmy," Debra said.

Tim was mid-step as she spoke, but he froze as his foot landed on the floor, the wood creaking as he planted it. His mother hadn't called him *Timmy* since he was Annie's age. "Are you okay? "

"I'm fine, Timmy," Mom said, again using the outdated variation of his name. "Just fine." With that, she turned to face her boy.

At first, Tim couldn't clearly see her from that distance, but a booming crack of thunder preceded a streak of lightning that, for a moment, lit up the room as if power had been restored. It was enough time for Tim to see the state his mother was in. The sight of her practically turned him to stone, paralyzing him as if she was Medusa herself.

On the surface, the woman by the window was in the shape of his mother, but everything about her was wrong. Her modest, pastel blue-and-yellow dress, one she had worn to church many times, was covered in bloody splotches. They were dark, but Tim knew what they were because the stains on her sleeves matched the bright crimson fluid that coated her hands, sluicing down the blade of the butcher knife she held in her right one, a steady drip plopping onto the floor, the sound mingling with the rain.

The image of his mother covered in blood was scary enough, but it was her expression that Tim found downright terrifying, especially framed by the soft light of the grinning jack-o'-lantern on the table next to her.

She smiled at him, a gesture meant to be reassuring, but the way the rictus grin stretched her cheeks looked unnatural. Despite Debra's generally uptight countenance, Tim had seen her smile plenty of times to convey a variety of emotions—amusement, joy, even mischief on occasion, yet he had never seen her smile like that. She looked like a Batman villain. But the most disturbing thing was her eyes. They were naturally brown, but they looked black. It may have been the sparse lighting, but they seemed impossibly dark, like they lacked a soul.

"Mom?" Tim addressed the shape of a woman yet again, still not recognizing her but not knowing how else to address her. "What... What happened?"

"I killed them, Timmy," she said as casually as if she was telling him what they were having for dinner.

"Who?"

"The people who were trying to hurt us, silly."

That didn't reassure him. Nothing about this made any sense. "I don't understand. Where's Molly?"

She didn't answer, only continued to smile. When she took a step toward him, his blood froze. "Timmy..." she started, but he cut her off.

"Where the fuck is Molly?" he shouted.

Debra halted, and her smile dropped. Her face took on a stern affect that, on the surface, looked more familiar but still felt wrong. Her eyes narrowed as she admonished him. "Timmy, that language is highly inappropriate. Come here *right now*."

Tim wanted to stay strong. This wasn't like getting caught cheating on a math test or even egging Mr. Wilbur's house. There were bad men outside. His father was hurt—maybe dead—his older sister was missing, and his mother was covered in someone's blood. This was life and death. His little sister and cousin were huddled in the closet, and he wanted to protect them like his father tried to protect him. He defiantly shook his head at the crazy woman's directive, fighting like hell to keep the tears from escaping.

"NOW!" she bellowed, stomping her foot.

That was enough to send the tears down his cheeks like a stuck candy bar dislodging from a vending machine. He did the opposite, stepping back rather than toward her. He had every intention of shouting to the younger children to run, but before he could open his mouth, there was a loud knock at the door.

Dad! he thought optimistically, feeling a sense of relief for the first time since he emerged from the closet.

His mother's expression remained furious, but her attention was divided. A second, louder knock made the door her priority. She stepped backward, keeping her eyes on her son until she reached the entrance, turning to look out the door window.

Tim saw her posture change as she practically

bounced with glee at whatever she saw outside. She quickly unlocked the door and moved to open it. It had to be Dad and Aunt Susan.

Maybe Mom had been telling the truth and she had killed the bad guys. Maybe she was acting so weird because stabbing them messed her up. That made sense. His mother had never killed anyone before, so of course it would have an effect on her.

She opened the door, and Tim's relieved sigh hit a roadblock on its way out of his lungs, nearly choking him as two men entered the house.

The first he recognized. It was the man from Mr. Wilbur's farm, the one who was pretending to be a cop. The other was a skinny man wearing a white disco suit that looked to be two sizes too big. The sight of them caused Tim's heart to sink. Even though the large one that had captured him and Mikey back at Wilbur's place wasn't with them, their presence almost certainly meant his dad and Aunt Susan were dead.

There was no time to mourn. He, Annie, and Franky were in grave danger. He realized it was even worse as his mother had one last surprise for him.

"Jack!" she exclaimed, throwing her arms around the man in uniform. He returned the hug, albeit not as enthusiastically as Debra. The skinny man seemed confused at the gesture, but Mom ignored him in favor of the man Tim now knew as Jack. "You're free? How did you get out?"

Tim was as perplexed as he was terrified, but he couldn't wait around to find out. Mom and the men were distracted, giving him an opportunity.

He quickly stepped back and gestured to Annie and Franky, who could still see him through the open closet door. He frantically waved his right arm, gesturing for them to come out while bringing his left index finger to his mouth, hoping desperately they understood he was telling them to move fast and quiet.

They exited their hiding spot, and Tim herded them away from his mother and the intruders, toward the kitchen, where they could escape via the back door. As he crossed the threshold into the next room, he again heard his mother's angry voice shout his name.

"Timmy!"

"Run!" Tim shouted to Annie and Franky.

The last thing he heard as they burst through the back door and into the torrential downpour was the man in the uniform giving an order.

"Oliver, retrieve the children."

CHAPTER 14

Susan knew something was very wrong as soon as she and Kevin emerged from the woods and back onto her brother's property. The front door was wide open, and while the glow from the fireplace and candles was visible, she couldn't see anyone inside.

"Kev?" she said in a way that asked, *Do you see this?*

He did, acknowledging it by pulling her arm from around his shoulders. She had supported him the whole way back from Dick Wilbur's farm, Kevin struggling with his injuries. She was afraid he would collapse since she was no longer helping keep him upright, but while he stumbled, he kept his balance.

Kevin righted himself and raised his shotgun. He turned to Susan and put a finger to his lips. She nodded her acknowledgment and lifted her rifle into a ready position. Kevin nodded, and the siblings entered the house, praying their loved ones were okay.

The first thing Susan noticed was the door to the closet where she had told Franky and Annie to hide was wide open, just like the front door. Panic washed over her as caution went out the window. "Franky!" she shouted as she rushed over and looked inside.

Her emotions were a mix of relief and anxiety when she saw it was empty, the diminishing candle providing enough light to see her son and his cousins were gone.

She stepped back and frantically surveyed the room, but other than the open doors, there was no sign anything was amiss, at least not at first. But as she scanned the area, she saw Kevin's attention was drawn to the floor by the table with the jack-o'-lantern. Keeping her weapon ready, she hurried to join him and choked as her breath caught in her throat when she saw the floor—more specifically, when she saw the small but fresh-looking puddle of blood.

"No," she muttered, not having intended to vocalize her distress but unable to stop herself.

"We don't know whose blood it is," Kevin said, answering the question that hung unspoken in the air between them. He tried to project a calm reassurance, but his voice was pained, both from his injuries and the stress of the situation.

Before either of them could suggest a next step, they were startled by a small noise coming from the kitchen. Brother and sister aimed their guns in tandem toward the darkened room.

They waited several beats before acting, giving anyone that may be hiding in the shadows the opportunity to announce themselves. When no one did, the siblings looked at each other. Kevin took a step toward the kitchen, cocking his head in the opposite direction, signaling Susan to stay behind him. She did as he instructed, and they headed into the unknown.

As they crossed into the room, the moonlight flowing in through the windows provided enough light to see. And Susan immediately wished she couldn't.

George's body was sprawled out on the floor in a pool of blood much larger than the small puddle by the jack-o'-lantern.

There was no need to check for a pulse, because a meat cleaver was embedded halfway into the young man's throat. His dead eyes bulged, and his tongue dangled obscenely from his gaping mouth, bloody saliva dripping from the tip, adding a foul mixture to the crimson pond beneath him.

Despite her revulsion at the sight and her fear of what further investigation may reveal, Susan's eyes followed the bloody trail that led away from Molly's dead boyfriend. It painted a gory path to the basement.

Susan turned to Kevin and saw his pained expression. It wasn't from his injuries. It was the fear that he would find his wife or his children in the same state as George. If Susan had a mirror, she knew her own face would be covered with a similar mask of dread. She prayed silently. *Please let Franky be okay.*

Kevin didn't look at her as he stepped over the corpse and pulled the door open. Susan's blood ran cold at what she saw when he did.

A lit candle rested on every third step, illuminating the passage to the house's lowest level. More fresh blood stained the steps. A lump formed in Susan's throat. It was too much to have seeped down from George's body. The blood was from someone else, and it was far too much to think that whoever that was would be alive. She didn't need medical training to know that.

Again, Kevin didn't coordinate with his sister as he started his descent. He wasn't charging headlong into the unknown, but he wasn't exercising the same level of caution, either.

Susan couldn't blame him. Her own concern for her son, nieces, and nephew was at an apex. She followed her brother down, careful to avoid the scarlet puddles creating a macabre hazard for the siblings.

Kevin pivoted to his left when he reached the bottom of the stairs, leading with his shotgun. She was two steps behind him when she saw his body stiffen in the dim light. A second later, he released a choked scream. "No!" He rushed forward, eschewing any remaining semblance of discretion.

Susan hurried to catch up and, as she turned the corner, saw the gruesome sight that had elicited Kevin's horror and anguish. She added her own scream to her brother's guttural sobs.

More candles were arranged in a circle. Inside the perimeter were four chairs lined in the same round pattern. Two were empty. Two were not.

Debra sat slumped in the seat to the right. Her head hung down, and her hair fell over her blood-soaked chest. The candles provided enough light to display the grisly scene, but it wasn't enough to tell if she was breathing.

Molly, the occupant of the other chair, was very much dead. Unlike her mother, her head hung back, the deep gash in her throat leaking the sparse amount of blood she had left. The wound gaped and made it look like her head was hanging on by a thread.

But the incision in her niece's neck looked like a paper cut compared to the one that stretched from her sternum to her naval. The flesh had been parted like a coat being unzipped, and jagged shards of her rib cage jutted from the cavernous wound. The poor girl's heart had been removed. Susan knew this because it lay on the floor in the middle of the circle atop a strange symbol painted in blood.

The symbol looked like a complex knot running through a jagged, inverted triangle with odd symbols surrounding it. It reminded her of horror movies she had seen where cultists would draw satanic symbols. But those were typically five-pointed stars inside a circle. This was an intentional drawing, but it was one she didn't recognize, though there was no doubt it was something evil.

Susan stood frozen, transfixed by the gruesome spectacle before her. She was numb and unsure how to act as her brother cried at the feet of the desecrated body of his daughter. If she could process the frenzied thoughts that snaked their way through her brain, she would feel guilty at her relief that Franky didn't appear to be there; but that didn't mean he was okay. She had to find him, but she didn't want to leave Kevin in his grief. It was during this contemplation that she heard a soft moan from Debra.

Kevin heard it too, because it pulled him out of his sorrowful stupor and spurred him to check on his wife.

"Debra!" he shouted as he shifted over to her, staying low so he could see her face, which still drooped. He gently cupped her chin and lifted her head.

Kevin was blocking Susan's view, so she couldn't see exactly what her sister-in-law did with the sudden jerky movement she made, but she heard a squelching thunk followed immediately by a different type of cry from her brother—pain.

Susan watched Kevin stagger back to his feet and slowly turn toward her. It was then that she saw the kitchen knife jutting out of his left eye socket. Fresh blood mingled with a milky fluid that flowed down his cheek and dripped off the bottom of his jaw. His mouth moved up and down like a ventriloquist's dummy, mimicking the act of speaking, but only choked, staccato grunts came out.

Debra rose from her chair, revealing herself to be uninjured. Her eyes were dark, and the smile that spread across her face looked inhuman and sinister. Susan screamed again. She could have asked why, but that would have been pointless. The woman creeping before her only wore her sister-in-law's form. They had never been particularly close, but this woman was not someone Susan recognized at all.

Susan stepped backward as Debra approached. Kevin stumbled and fell to his knees, somehow keeping the upper half of his body straight. He tried to lift his arms, intending to extricate the blade from his ruined eye, but he could only raise them halfway before they fell limply to his sides as he swayed, threatening to fall over at any second.

As the monster who looked like his wife stepped forward and reached around, cupping his forehead and drawing his head back underneath her bosom, stroking his hair in a faux loving gesture, Susan felt a presence behind her. Before she could act, an arm snaked around her throat, choking off another scream before she could release it. It was only then that she remembered she had the rifle, a fact she had somehow forgotten in the chaos. She tried to raise it, but the assailant behind her tightened their grip on her throat, causing it to loosen enough for them to snatch the rifle from her and toss it aside.

The hand that relieved her of her weapon disappeared. It didn't come back into view, but she heard the familiar sound of a pistol hammer clicking back and felt cold steel press against her temple. A man's voice came from behind her.

"Best to just keep still. Don't try to be a hero. He's already dead."

Susan knew it. As much as she didn't want to believe it, she knew her brother was going to die. She watched helplessly as Debra gripped the knife handle and violently pulled it out, sending more blood and fluid splattering at Susan's feet. She cried as she watched her sister-in-law take the knife and plunge it into Kevin's jugular, twisting it before yanking it out and stabbing him in the throat again.

And again.

And again.

And again.

CHAPTER 15

Tim kept his sister and cousin in front of him as they exited the woods. It was hard for him since he could easily have outrun both of them. But he needed to make sure they were safe, and staying behind them was the only way to do that.

Both young ones had frozen when they first ran into the kitchen, horrified at George's dead body sprawled out on the floor. Tim had to shove them out the back door and keep them moving as they ran toward the woods.

Halfway between the house and the tree line, he heard footsteps, accompanied by maniacal laughter, behind them. He allowed himself enough of a head turn to see the weird, skinny man wearing the disco suit running after them, his arms flailing as he gave chase.

Fortunately for Tim and the children, he was familiar with the woods, and he took a path he knew was dense with trees and had several large rocks and ditches that would provide cover. He found the one he was looking for with little effort and pulled Annie and Franky in close as they hid from their pursuer, wrapping his arms around them and covering their mouths as the rain pounded down on them.

He felt them tense as he heard the man's footsteps approach, slowing from a run to a deliberate walk, no doubt surveying the surroundings to find the trio.

"Little pigs, little pigs, come the fuck out," the man said in a raspy voice that dripped with malice. "I promise I won't hurt you." That last statement was followed by a chuckle, as no one in their right mind would believe that. "How about you just give me the little girl? I'll let the two of you go about your business if you do that."

Tim felt anger bubble in him. He knew he couldn't take the man one on one, but he wanted to kill him for having the temerity to threaten his little sister.

"You little fuckers are no fun," the man said, his voice carrying the tone and tenor of impatience. "The harder you make this on me, the worse it's going to be on you."

Tim felt Annie and Franky shaking in his grip. It was mainly rain that wetted his hands, but he knew they were crying, too, trying their best to keep it under control.

The man fell silent. Tim wanted to look, but he didn't know if the creep was on the other side of the rock or somewhere down the path. If it was the former, they wouldn't be able to get away. All he could do was wait.

The shrill bark of a coyote came from somewhere nearby, sending a bolt of ice up Tim's spine. While the presence of a different kind of predator was another threat, it served to assist the trio of frightened children in revealing their antagonist's position.

"What the fuck was that?" the man said to himself.

Tim could tell from the sound of his voice that the guy was farther down the path, going toward the Wilbur farm. The coyote sang its song again, that time even closer, and the man followed up with a, "Fuck this!" before Tim heard him run, his footfalls quickly fading in the opposite direction.

"We gotta go," he whispered, acting fast to motivate the younger kids, uncovering their mouths and grabbing their hands again, running as fast as he could with them back toward his house. His mother and the other man were still there as far as he knew, but there were other places to hide, and better to take a chance at a more familiar locale than to head in the direction of the maniac chasing them. Not to mention the coyotes.

So they were back on his family's property. He could see the front door was wide open, but that was the last place he was going to go. Instead, he nudged Annie and Franky toward the left side of the property, in the direction of the barn.

To their credit, the younger kids were doing their best despite their fear and the rain slowing them down. When they reached the barn, he moved around them and pulled the door open, ushering them inside before slipping in himself. Once on the other side, he took a moment to take a breath and feel the relief of being out of the rain before pushing the door shut.

"Is he gone?" Franky asked meekly, his voice barely audible.

"I want Mommy," Annie said.

The mention of his mother made Tim want to vomit. He still couldn't believe she was a part of this, whatever *this* was. The thing he didn't get was that she had obviously killed George—maybe Molly too—yet she seemed surprised to see the men from Mr. Wilbur's farm show up at the door. She knew them but didn't know they were there. None of it made any sense. Was she hypnotized like the magicians on TV did?

Tim's breathing slowed to a manageable level, and he looked around the barn. He saw two things straight away he thought could help—one to hide and one to defend.

Without explaining, he ran around Annie and Franky and grabbed a pitchfork hanging in a stall next to the hay bales. With the weapon in hand, he turned to the younger kids, whose eyes were locked on him. He pointed to the rear of the barn, where a wood ladder was affixed to the beam leading to the loft where more hay was stored.

"There," he ordered.

Annie and Franky exchanged a glance, and Tim could tell they were nervous about climbing the ladder. He ran to them and crouched to look them in the eyes.

"I know you're scared, guys," he said softly, "but we'll be safe up there." He paused, knowing his next statement was more optimistic than he felt. "We can wait there until Dad and Aunt Susan get back."

Annie looked up at the loft, and Franky's eyes followed. They were still hesitant. But a voice from outside spurred them to take the chance.

"Where the fuck are you?" the man in the disco suit shouted. It was no longer the sing-song playful tone he had previously. He was pissed. Tim rushed back to the front. There was a small knothole in the right barn door, so Tim was able to look out. He saw the man, angry and wet, the oversized suit clinging to his skinny frame, heading right for them.

"Go! Now!" he ordered, giving them a shove to get them started.

Annie and Franky ran. Annie started climbing the ladder first, having been up there before, albeit not often. Franky hesitated at the bottom, but Tim lifted him onto the first step, getting him started. His cousin moved after that, his pace too slow not to exacerbate the young teen's anxiety. But he couldn't push him any harder or he may just lose him entirely.

C'mon. C'mon. C'mon, Tim urged in his mind.

Finally, Franky crossed the threshold to the second floor, and Tim hurried behind him, his foot stepping off the ladder just as the barn doors flung violently open.

"There," he whispered, pointing to an arrangement of hay bales in the corner. Annie and Franky did as they were told and ducked behind them and out of sight as Tim saw the man enter the barn, murder in his eyes.

"I'm going to fucking gut you," the man said through gritted teeth. "And that's just the start."

Tim followed his sister and cousin and ducked behind the hay bales. Gripping the pitchfork tightly, he shut his eyes and prayed the man wouldn't come up there. The ladder was a fixture, so they couldn't pull it up and block his access. But there was nothing else they could do.

The man must have calmed himself, because the next time he spoke his voice was more even. "I saw your little friend at the other farm," he said. "Wallace ripped his guts out real good. He was a mighty fine sacrifice."

Tim felt tears seep out of his closed eyes, the image of Mikey's mutilated corpse as clear as if it was painted on the inside of his eyelids.

"It doesn't have to be that for you," he continued. "I mean, I'm going to tear your organs out, but if you come out now, I'll make sure you're dead before I do. I'll make it quick. Scout's honor."

Annie let out a whimper. Tim tried to cover her mouth, but it was too late.

The man went silent for several interminable seconds before he made another sound. Only that time, he wasn't speaking; he was singing. Tim didn't know the song, but the lyrics chilled him. Especially when he referred to a *Stairway to Heaven.*

The man's off-key song continued as his footsteps crackled in the hay that littered the floor, getting farther away from the entrance and closer to the back of the barn—the back of the barn where the ladder was located.

Any notion that the psychopath would go away disappeared as Tim heard him step up the ladder. The motion grew louder as he climbed, taking his time ascending to the loft. He had stopped singing the words but continued to hum the melody as he reached the upper level.

Tim positioned himself in front of Annie and Franky, gripping the pitchfork and ready to stab when the wicked man eventually reached them. For the moment, however, he had stopped moving.

"Last chance, boy," the man said, his voice even closer. "Last chance to die quick."

Tim couldn't let him find them. He knew the man had figured out where they were hiding. The only chance he had was the element of surprise. And the only way he could surprise the man was by doing the last thing the guy expected. Tim took a breath and charged. Bursting from behind the hay, he yelled at the top of his lungs and aimed the pitchfork in the approximate direction of the man. He misjudged. Badly.

The man was already off to the side, and the shit-eating grin on his face told Tim he was in trouble. He tried to adjust mid-lunge, but it was awkward and the man easily caught the pitchfork by the handle and used it, and Tim's momentum, to toss him aside. Tim hit the ground hard, his wind fleeing from his lungs.

Trying to compose himself, the boy attempted to sit up but was met by a hard kick to his chest, knocking him back down. The man took his time, his expression taunting, as he first stood over Tim, then crouched onto his sternum, pinning the teen's arms between his skinny legs.

Tim struggled, getting his head off the ground, but the man punched him in the face. A blinding white flash preceded a jolt of pain, followed by a sudden numbness on the left side of his face. His mouth felt wet and he tasted blood. He had never been punched in the face before, and it was so much worse than it looked on TV.

He groaned and rolled his head to the side. Even though he didn't try to get up, the man punched him again, that one landing just below his right eye, forcing it closed. Was he going to get beaten to death?

"I told you I would have made it quick, boy," the man said, squeezing his legs together, constricting Tim's body and driving more air from him. "But you can die knowing that it'll be so much worse for the little ones." The psycho reached into his pocket and pulled out a wooden handle, not even taking a breath before he extended the sharp blade embedded in it. "Found this knife at your neighbor's house. Figured he didn't need it no more."

The man traced the knife down Tim's cheek and under his jaw, resting the tip on the boy's throat. While it wasn't pressed hard enough to cut, he could feel how sharp it was, knew his flesh wouldn't stand a chance against it. The maniac cackled as he pulled the knife away, flipping its position in his hand, ready to stab. He blew his pending victim a kiss and raised it high.

Tim squeezed his eyes shut, resigned to his fate.

He expected to feel his skin getting pierced but it never came. He opened his eyes and saw the man was still straddling him, but the knife was no longer in a position to strike. Rather, his arms were reaching around his back as if he was trying to remove something. It wasn't immediately clear to Tim until the man stood and turned.

The pitchfork was sticking out of his back. It hadn't gone in too far, a combination of the dull points and the eight-year-old's lack of strength, but it was impaled deep enough to hurt. Blood blossomed around the teeth of the tool, a crimson flower blooming on the back of his white jacket.

The man stumbled forward and slightly to the left, where Tim could see Franky standing frozen in front of him. His cousin must have been the one to stab him, but he wasn't strong enough to embed the weapon to a depth where it could do real damage. Tim knew he didn't have time to rest because the man, while staggered, could easily get to the small boy and make good on his vile threats.

Tim used every bit of strength and will to get up and again rush the man. That time, he was on target and able to grab the pitchfork. He yanked it back, pulling the psycho away from his cousin. The man yelped in pain as Tim whirled him around one hundred eighty degrees so he was away from Franky. With the younger boy clear, Tim threw all his weight behind the thrust, driving the pitchfork deeper and knocking the man to his stomach. He pushed forward one more time and drove the pitchfork even farther into his opponent.

Tim fell to his side, landing on the man's left. When he saw how close he was, he rolled away, but his energy was waning. His breath was ragged, and in the place his face didn't sting, it felt like it had swelled to three times its size. But at least he wasn't dead like the other guy.

Again, his assessment was wrong. Annie screamed,

and the man groaned as he got back to his feet. Tim saw four bloody circles on the front of his shirt, but the prongs weren't all the way through. Still, he had to have hit something important. Right? The man was wobbly, and blood was pouring from his mouth. How he was mobile Tim didn't know.

"Fucking... kill you... you..." The man stepped forward to make good on his threat, but he didn't account for the weight of the pitchfork in his back, and gravity took it from there. He took one step back and almost righted himself, but his spine was bent too far backward and it looked as if he hung in the air for a second before he toppled to the floor of the barn, a stunted groan and wet crunch accompanying his impact.

Tim crawled to the edge and looked down. The man was lying on his side, but from the look of him, he landed on the handle before toppling over. The prongs protruded clearly out of his front. His head hung unnaturally as his neck must have also broken when he landed.

Tim rolled on his back and saw Franky standing over him. The boy had his hand out to help him up. If Tim's face muscles worked, he may have smiled as he accepted it. Struggling to sit up, then willing himself to his feet, he saw Annie join them.

"What do we do now?" she asked.

Tim didn't want to leave, but they had just made a lot of noise and there was still his mother and the other guy in their house. And the big man at Mr. Wilbur's farm with Dad and, maybe, Aunt Susan. They had to get out of there, and their best chance was to head to the road and hope a car passed by to help them.

"We're going to get out of here," Tim said. "Stay close and follow me."

The trio climbed down from the loft. Tim went first, keeping an eye on the dead maniac below them. He hadn't moved an inch since he fell, but Tim wasn't taking any chances. He stepped down and stayed as a barrier between the kids and the body. When they were clear, he again took the lead and led Annie and Franky to the door. He pushed it open and started toward the road.

He was only a step out of the barn when he felt a large hand on the back of his neck. It was a feeling he had felt only a short time earlier at Mr. Wilbur's farm. He heard Annie and Franky scream as his feet left the ground. Against his will, he was turned around and found himself face to face with the big man he had last seen beating his father. Dad must have gotten a few licks in, because there was a bloody gash on the side of the man's forehead and one side of his face was caked with drying blood, a face that remained emotionless as his grip on Tim's throat tightened. Before he completely lost his ability to speak, he used all the force his vocal cords could muster to give one last instruction to the children.

"Run!"

Immediately after the words left his mouth, Tim felt his head get violently jerked around. He didn't have time to process that it was too far or exactly what the loud snapping noise was, but the last thing he saw before everything went black was Franky and Annie running away, screaming.

CHAPTER 16

Susan knew she couldn't overpower Debra and the wicked man, but she wasn't going to make it easy on them. She thrashed and clawed and kicked as the depraved duo tied her to another chair, one outside of the circle with the strange symbol. She felt a length of thick rope tighten around her sternum, trapping her arms at her sides, courtesy of the unknown man.

Debra worked on her feet but was having difficulty. Susan got off a good kick that connected with her sister-in-law's lip, knocking her off-balance and onto her ass. The yelp she let out upon landing was a mix of pain and anger. Susan gave her a *fuck you* grin when Debra got her bearings enough to make eye contact.

Debra raged as she got up, and she lunged at Susan, belting the captive woman with an open hand slap. It stung for sure, causing her to bite her lip, drawing blood. But tragically, Susan was used to being struck by someone bigger and stronger than her sister-in-law. So while there *was* pain, there wasn't the shock of being struck.

She quickly pivoted her head and spat a bloody wad of phlegm, splattering Debra's cheek, flashing a sardonic smile in the process that sent Debra into a blind rage.

The crazed woman picked up the butcher knife she used to murder Kevin and charged Susan with the weapon held high. Susan's smile vanished and she braced herself, anticipating the same fate as her brother. But the knife didn't fall.

The man had intercepted Debra's killing blow. He gripped her wrist, preventing her from using her weapon. She looked at him with confusion, while the man projected an aura of calm resolve.

"Jack?" she asked, inadvertently revealing her partner's name.

"Don't get distracted, Debra," he said in an even tone. "She's not your objective tonight."

Debra's posture relaxed, and the man Susan now knew as Jack let go of her wrist. Debra's anger dissipated, and a look of confusion replaced it. "I-I was going to do as you said. I just didn't realize you would be here for it."

What the hell is she talking about?

"Believe me, I am just as surprised as you are," Jack replied, sounding genuine. "Ba'al sent a dark angel to free me so I can be here with you tonight."

"What the fuck is going on?" Susan interrupted. "How do you know each other?"

Anger again flashed in Debra's eyes as she raised her arm, preparing to backhand her captive. Again, Jack grabbed her wrist and gently pushed it down. "It's okay, Debra. I'm sure Miss ..."

He paused, offering Susan the opportunity to introduce herself. She didn't take it, so her sister-in-law did.

"Her name is Susan. She's Kevin's sister."

"Ah!" Jack said with amusement. "A real family affair!"

"Yes!" Debra added excitedly. "She *is* family. She can be part of the ritual!"

"Patience, Debra," Jack said. "It's not about blood. It's about sacrifice. I get the sense you don't really care for this woman. Her death would not serve Ba'al's purpose."

"I understand, Jack," Debra replied, looking deflated.

"Who is Ba'al?" Susan asked.

The question seemed to stir something in Jack, because he lit up at the mention of his master's name.

"Ba'al is who we serve," Jack answered without hesitation. "He's gone by many names over the years but, most prominently, Ba'al Berith as he was known to the Canaanites. He is a great duke of Jinnestan, home of the djinn. Are you familiar with the term?"

"No," Susan said, tamping down the urge to be flippant. It was better to keep him talking because she was terrified of what was going to happen once he stopped.

Jack chuckled as if the words he was using were as

common as *saints* and *sinners*. "A djinn is what you would refer to as a genie. They don't live in lamps that you rub to summon them, but they do grant wishes to those that are loyal." His voice lowered, and he spoke in an almost seductive tone. "Fulfill desires."

"How does he grant wishes?" Susan asked.

"Ba'al does not share the source of his abilities with me. But he is a powerful lord of demons, commanding twenty-six legions while also serving as the chief secretary of hell. He sees all—past, present, and future, and can turn metal to gold. His influence is vast, and for those who follow him, the possibilities are limitless."

"What does that have to do with my brother's family?" Susan asked, getting choked up as she saw the lifeless husks that used to be her brother and niece tied to chairs in the satanic circle.

Jack answered as casually as he would tell you what he had for breakfast. "Years ago, Ba'al saved me from myself. To repay him, I made it my life's mission to recruit new disciples to his cause. I met Debra here through her church's outreach program to Pine Hill. These lovely women would come and sit with the mentally disturbed, reading to them, spreading the wretched gospel of the Creator."

"I was so foolish," Debra chimed in, looking legitimately embarrassed. "So foolish."

"What Debra didn't realize was that I was not disturbed. I am as sane as you, Susan."

Not a fucking chance, she thought as Jack continued.

"At first, Debra was surprised when I challenged her long-held concepts of good and evil. I'd even venture to say she was downright angry with me. But she persisted in trying to get me to see the light. And I persisted in showing her the truth of the world. Eventually, she realized that the man in the robe behind the pulpit was shoveling shit down her throat every week. She pledged herself to Ba'al."

"I do, Jack! I pledge myself!"

"That you do, sweetheart," Jack said to Debra, without taking his eyes off Susan. "That's why I arranged this test for you tonight."

"What test?" Susan asked.

"To be a disciple of Ba'al, you must prove yourself. This can look different depending on the person. For Debra here, her initiation was to unshackle herself from the heathens she called family."

As the situation became clear, Susan felt herself flush with anger. If it were humanly possible to break free of her restraints, she would kill Debra with her bare hands. But this wasn't a movie, and she had no obvious way out of her predicament.

"So you broke out to help her kill my brother and his kids?"

That really amused Jack, and he let out a hearty laugh! "Not at all!" he said between deranged giggles. "I just delivered the instructions. I had no plans to actually be here. That was Ba'al's grace."

"What the hell does that mean?"

"Ba'al sent a dark angel to free me from my confinement on this the festival of Samhain."

The questions would be irritating if they weren't the only thing buying her time. "Samhain?" she asked.

"Halloween. The Celtic tribes celebrated it as Samhain. At the time of the end of the harvest, the veil that separates the world of the living and the dead is at its thinnest. This allows spirits from the Underworld to cross over and possess the living. That is why people used to leave baskets of goodies on their doorsteps—to appease the spirits, a *treat* to avoid an evil *trick*."

"An evil spirit broke you out?" She thought the question may spur another wicked laugh, but Jack was stone-cold serious.

"A dark angel," he repeated. "There was a patient at the hospital. He never spoke, but I knew there was something inside of him. And tonight, when he broke down my door and freed me, along with the others, I knew he was sent by Ba'al so I could come here to witness Debra's rebirth into his ministry."

Before she could think of another question to continue buying time, the sound of heavy footsteps came from the floor above. While Susan hoped it would be someone that could aid her, the air was thick with dread, and she knew whoever was upstairs would not provide her the help she needed.

The three of them turned their attention to the stairs as they saw the large figure descend into the room with them, heavy thuds accompanying each footfall.

Susan was in shock at the sight of him. It was the large man she had shot at the neighbor's farm. The entire side of his face was caked with dried blood from the gash in his temple. She had grazed him good, but it hadn't been enough to do more than superficial damage. But she didn't dwell too long on the man's injuries. What was more terrifying was what he carried.

In his right hand, he dragged the body of a skinny man wearing a white leisure suit with a pitchfork sticking out of his back. The prongs were embedded deep, and blood bloomed around the metal, staining much of the jacket. But it was the corpse slung over his shoulder that spurred her to scream—her nephew, Tim.

The boy's head was twisted almost all the way around, and a gruesome protrusion stretched the skin on his neck, which had bled to a harsh shade of purple. The thirteen-year-old's eyes were wide, frozen in the horror of the final, violent moments of his life.

Much of her cry was grief for the boy, but there was also the twisting dread of uncertainty. Tim had been with the younger kids, with Franky. If he was dead, where was her son?

The large man released the skinny corpse outside of the circle but kept Tim hoisted on his shoulder. Jack looked perplexed. Debra had no reaction at all to her son's death.

The evil fucking bitch has really lost her mind.

"Wallace," Jack said, addressing the big man. "What happened to Oliver?"

Wallace slapped Tim's back.

"The boy managed to take him down. Interesting. Oh, well. Oliver was never the strongest of my disciples. He had his uses, but I'm not going to lose sleep over his passing. I'm assuming you killed the boy?"

Wallace stood stone-faced, offering only a slight nod.

Jack sighed. "That's...problematic. Debra needed to sacrifice her entire family."

"I would have!" Debra said, frantically positioning herself in front of Jack. "My intent was there. I would not have hesitated."

"Alas, we'll never know," Jack said, an exaggerated air of disappointment in his words.

"But ...But ..." Debra stammered. "I can prove myself in other ways. Just tell me. Tell me what you want, Jack!"

The desperation in her voice was pathetic, and Susan had no pity for her.

"Why don't you sacrifice yourself?" Susan offered in an acidic tone. "Cut your own throat, you fucking bitch."

Debra screeched and lunged at her again, and again, Jack grabbed her and pulled her back, slapping her hard across her face, stunning her into silence. "Let that be your last outburst, Debra!"

Her mouth moved, but no words came out.

"You will have your chance to prove yourself." He turned to Wallace. "Where are the little ones?"

Wallace used his now free hand to point upstairs.

"Are they in the house?" Jack asked for clarification. When Wallace shook his head, Jack said, "Put young Timothy in one of the empty chairs, then go get them and bring them back. *Alive.*"

Wallace nodded and did as instructed, setting Tim's body down in the chair next to what was left of Molly. Unfettered, he turned and left the basement.

"Leave them alone, you bastard!" Susan screamed.

Her words, unsurprisingly, fell on deaf ears as the big man's steps grew more distant before they heard the back door open then swing closed.

Even Jack was ignoring her, instead addressing his acolyte. "When Wallace returns, you will complete the last sacrifice of your daughter," he said, before turning to Susan. "Then you will kill the other little one and see if Ba'al accepts the substitute."

"NO!" Susan bellowed. That time, Jack slapped her, and that time, it hurt. Badly.

"What if Ba'al doesn't accept it?" Debra asked nervously.

"He'll tell us what to do next. But we won't know until the boy is dead."

Susan felt a surge of panic. The two eight-year-olds were out God knew where with no one to help them. If this Wallace person caught them, they would be helpless. She prayed frantically in her mind. *Please. Please. Please. Don't let him find them. Please send me help. I need help.*

She didn't expect to have her prayers answered at all, let alone so quickly.

A flood of light entered the room from the windows facing the front of the property. Headlights.

Someone was there.

CHAPTER 17

I fucking knew it, Charles thought as pulled up to his brother-in-law's farmhouse.

As suspected, Susan's car was parked next to Kevin's pickup truck. His darling wife was nothing if not predictable. She just had to go and involve her family in their business. Her brother was always a smarmy prick as far as Charles was concerned. He better watch his fucking mouth when it came to his and Susan's marriage.

Charles killed the engine and stepped out of the car, thankful the rain had mostly stopped at that point. As he walked up to the house, something felt off. For one, the inside was dark with a few flickering points of light, probably candles. The power being out wasn't what he was expecting but made sense given the storm, so that by itself wasn't enough to raise the alarm. The front door being ajar, however, was. He slowed and flicked the snap on his holster, hovering his hand above the butt of his service revolver.

He pulled the small flashlight from his utility belt and held it in his other hand, waving the beam around the area, looking for anything else out of the ordinary. Sure enough, he found it, and it was enough to spur him to draw his pistol and assume a full defensive stance.

The tires on Susan's car were flat. He trained the light on the front passenger side and saw the rubber was crudely slashed. Switching the beam to its rear counterpart, he saw the same thing. Charles sidestepped slowly to the other side of the vehicle and saw both tires in the same condition. It was the same for the ones on the passenger side of Kevin's truck. He didn't bother looking at the driver's side—both cars were disabled no matter what. He raised his pistol and flashlight and crept up the porch, pushing the door open all the way to gain entry.

Inside, he found further evidence that something was amiss. He cleared both sides of the room as he was trained to. There was no one in sight, but there was a small puddle of what looked like blood pooled under a table where a grinning jack-o'-lantern mocked him.

What the fuck? he thought to himself as he proceeded toward an open closet next to the kitchen entryway. He hadn't been up there much, but he had visited enough times to have a general idea of the house's layout. Charles examined the closet and found it empty, but a small, extinguished candle, a doll, and some army men were on the floor. Where was his son?

"Franky?" Charles whispered a little louder than he

wanted to, but he needed the boy to hear him if he was near. "Franky, it's Dad. You can come out." There was no reply, and Charles felt the familiar anger constrict his body. The little shit never listened.

He breathed deep and steadied himself. There was something seriously wrong here. Once he resolved it, he would give Franky a good talking to. And he would give Susan her medication. Judging by her recent actions, he would have to significantly up the dose to ensure it never happened again.

Charles scanned the living room one last time to double-check. As he was getting ready to move on, he heard the sound of a woman crying coming from the kitchen. Susan. He raised his flashlight and gun and stepped inside. He cleared his right sightline first and found nothing. On his left, he made a gruesome discovery.

A young man he had never seen before, he couldn't have been more than nineteen or twenty, lay dead on the ground in a massive pool of blood with a meat cleaver jammed deep into his neck. And he wasn't alone.

His sister-in-law knelt next to the upper part of the boy's body, crying. Her own dress was covered in copious amounts of blood. Her hair, usually tied back in a tight ponytail or bun, hung loosely over the front of her face. She wasn't looking at him. Charles didn't know if she was even aware that he walked in.

"Debra," he said loud enough to get her attention. She looked up, and Charles didn't even recognize her. He would never claim he was close with Susan's family, but the woman in front of him may as well have been a stranger. She could be traumatized by having found the body, but Charles had seen people in similar situations throughout his career as a sheriff's officer. People liked to say that Woodbury was a quiet town where nothing ever happened, but there had been enough accidents and the occasional murder for Charles to know what people looked like when they were faced with death. That wasn't the look Debra had, and it kept his guard up.

"Charles?" she asked in a strange tone.

"What happened here?"

"Oh!" she said, getting to her feet. He noticed one hand was behind her back. "Thank God you're here!" She took a step toward him.

Charles drew back the hammer on the revolver, halting her in her tracks. "Stay there, Debra," he ordered.

"Charles," she said, trying to sound innocent. "What are you doing?"

"You need to tell me just what the fuck is going on here. Right now!"

"We...we were attacked," she said. "A big man broke in and tried to hurt us. He killed my daughter's boyfriend." She gestured toward the body to emphasize he was who she was referencing.

"Where's Susan and Franky?"

"They're in the basement. Kevin told them to hide when the intruder broke in."

"Okay. So where's Kevin?"

"Our phone isn't working. He went next door to Dick Wilbur's farm. Dick has a CB radio, you see. He can use it to call the police."

"What's behind your back?"

"What do you mean?" Debra asked.

"Let me see your hands. Both of them."

"Charles, I'm a victim here. You're being rude."

"Hands. Now."

A twisted grin spread across Debra's face. Even to someone like Charles, who was not a good man, it looked evil. She slowly brought her hand from behind her back and showed her brother-in-law the blood-stained butcher knife she had been hiding.

Charles swallowed hard. "I'm going to ask you one more time, Debra. Where the hell is my family?"

"Susan's in the basement. I wasn't lying."

"And Franky?"

"He'll be back soon. Why don't you come downstairs, and we'll talk about it? You'll understand better once we're down there."

"Drop the knife."

She did as instructed, opening her fingers and letting the blade fall to the ground, the metal clanking against the bloody tile as it landed. She raised her other hand and spread the fingers as well, showing him she was no longer armed.

"Happy?"

Charles didn't answer that. He flicked his wrist on the hand holding the gun to gesture to Debra to move. The grin never left her face as she turned and started down the stairs. He followed her, keeping the gun trained on her.

She moved down the stairs with a steady gait. She

didn't give off the appearance of trying to run, but if she made any sudden moves, he would drop her. There was enough here that he would be justified. He would claim it looked like she killed the boy if he had to take her out.

She reached the bottom of the stairs and spoke to someone off to her side. "Jack, dear. We have company."

Charles followed down and around the corner and found a house of horrors.

Susan was tied to a chair. Her eyes bugged when she saw her husband. Clearly, she was hoping for a cavalry, but this one was not her ideal one.

A man wearing a security guard's uniform stood behind her holding a forty-five-caliber pistol to her head. It looked like one of Kevin's. Charles had gone shooting with his brother-in-law on a few occasions early on, before his relationship with his wife and her family deteriorated.

Speaking of Kevin, his mutilated corpse was tied to a chair, away from Susan. It was in the middle of a bloody circle painted on the floor with some fucked-up-looking symbols.

There were three other chairs. One was empty. On the others sat the bodies of two of Kevin's kids. Molly was ripped open from gut to gullet, and Tim looked like his neck had been broken. Charles didn't have any great love for those kids, but it was still a messed-up sight to see.

Another body, a skinny man in a leisure suit, lay off to the side, a pitchfork protruding from his back. The pungent odor of freshly spilled blood permeated the air, invading Charles's nostrils.

"Jesus Christ," he muttered.

"Charles!" Susan choked out, knowing damn well the devil she knew was preferable to...whoever the fuck those people were. "Franky's out there."

"Welcome, Charles...," the man in the security guard's uniform started.

He didn't have time to finish his greeting as Charles put a bullet directly between his eyes. The projectile exited the back of the man's head, spraying blood across the jarred preserves that lined the shelves behind him. He fell backward, his head smacking against the concrete inconsequentially, since he was dead before he hit the ground.

Both Susan and Debra screamed at the turn of events, albeit for different reasons—Susan from the sheer shock of it, and Debra because she was clearly in on something with that psychopath.

"Bastard!" Debra screamed as she ran at Charles. It was an action borne of pure emotion and not any type of actual strategy, as she was unarmed and Charles still had his pistol. She barely made it two steps before he shot her three times in the chest. Each bullet tore through her dress, blood bursting from the entry points. She stumbled and fell to her knees. Charles was prepared to shoot her again, but she only stayed there for a moment, swaying until she crashed face-first onto the floor.

"Fucking whackos," Charles said.

"Charles!" Susan yelled. "Untie me! We have to get Franky!"

He turned his attention to his wife and saw her

struggling against her bonds, a manic look in her eyes.

"Where is he?" Charles asked.

"He's in the woods!" she said frantically. "These are escaped mental patients! There's another one still after him and Annie."

Charles turned and looked toward the stairs, more contemplating than actually trying to see anything.

"Charles!" Susan shouted again, breaking his concentration. "Untie me!"

Charles looked back at his wife. He smiled, and not in a comforting way. "Wait here, sweetheart. I'll go get Franky. Then we can all go home."

CHAPTER 18

"Charles!" Susan screamed as she heard her husband exit the house on the floor above, leaving her to sit and wait in the graveyard that used to be her brother's basement.

While Debra and her two friends here no longer posed a threat, there was still the other one that went after Franky and Annie. Even if Charles could somehow take him down—and that was in doubt, given that neither Kevin nor a bullet to the head had been successful in that regard—she still had the problem of her husband. She had come here to flee Charles and his abuse. If he brought her back home, it would be worse than ever. He may even kill her himself. That was something she had never really considered. Yes, he had hit her, but would he end her life? She would have said no, but having seen how casually he shot Jack and Debra, she wasn't so sure.

She knew she had to free herself if she had any chance of survival. She looked around for something to help cut the rope but saw nothing obvious. Maybe she could just throw herself back and break the chair. Wasn't that what they did in movies? But that didn't seem possible. The chair felt very sturdy, and she couldn't get any type of real momentum because of the way she was tied up. Without something to cut it, she wasn't getting free.

She craned her neck as far as she could and saw the shelving behind her. That was when she saw the only chance she had.

Thankful that her hands were only restrained at her sides and not tied together, she gripped either end of the seat and used her legs to push off the ground in a small bunny-hop motion. It had the desired effect as the chair moved a couple inches back. She repeated the process, trying to maneuver toward the shelves while also navigating around Jack's corpse. It was much harder than she would have thought. Sweat slicked her body, and her lungs burned as she slowly made her way to the back of the room while tied to the chair. Her aching legs throbbed, and her fingers cramped from the monumental effort.

When she was finally close enough to the shelves, she thrust herself back again, rattling the jars that lined them. One fell backward, but it didn't hit the ground. She thrust again, rattling them further. A third time finally sent most of them tumbling from their perch and onto the ground, shattering and spreading glass across the concrete.

As tough as it had been to get that far, the toughest part was still to come.

Susan rocked back and forth until she finally went tumbling toward the shattered jars littering the floor. She did her best to fall in a way to minimize the damage, but while she avoided most of the glass, her shoulder smacked into the ground, shooting a bolt of agony across it for a split second before it went numb. The landing confirmed her initial theory that the chair would not break. But it did crack, which served to loosen the binds a bit, allowing her some maneuverability with her arms.

She only allowed herself the briefest of moments to feel the pain before she started wriggling around, bringing the anchor that was the wooden chair with her. She felt around for a shard that would work. Her fingers found one the hard way, and she felt the sting of her flesh being parted as she picked it up, gritting her teeth as she fought her instinct to drop it.

Maneuvering her hand around despite the numbness in her shoulder and the searing pain from her gashed fingers, she brought the shard to the center of her abdomen, where she transferred it to her other hand. Thankfully, she was a lefty and the injuries were worse on her right side. With her dominant hand in control, she brought the sizeable shard to the ropes and started sawing.

She didn't know how long she worked, but it seemed like forever with no progress. She wouldn't give up, but her arms were bathed in agony and the glass was cutting into her good hand at that point. Her body's physical capacity looked as if it was going to wane despite her desire to save her son. But she felt the rope loosen. The progress spurred her forward, and soon the strands parted as the first loop separated. She immediately went to work on the next one, feeling the sweat sting her eyes as she put everything she had into escaping. When the second loop fell away, it was enough for her to wriggle out of the rest, freeing herself from the chair.

She rolled to her stomach and pushed herself to her feet, fighting the urge to just lay down and pass out after the Herculean effort she had just undertaken to escape. As she stood, she saw Kevin's shotgun resting on the wall behind his body. The twenty-two hadn't been enough to stop the man Jack referred to as Wallace, but a twelve-gauge slug would blow his fucking head off. That should do the trick.

She limped over to the mud-caked weapon, her legs still acclimating to her newfound freedom. Retrieving it, she went right for the stairs, adrenaline propelling her forward to save her son.

CHAPTER 19

“Come on!” Franky shouted to Annie, who was slowing down as they weaved their way through the trees.

“Wait!” Annie said, panic in her voice. “I don’t know where we are.”

“Don’t you know these woods?” Franky asked.

Annie shook her head. “No, I...I never liked it out here. Tim was the one who knew where to go.”

Franky looked around, trying to think of what direction they should go. He had no idea what to look for. He grew up in the suburbs, and while he had been to his uncle’s farm plenty of times, the surrounding forest wasn’t familiar to him at all. As he frantically tried to figure out what to do next, he heard rustling in the trees behind him. Annie heard it too, because she yelped.

The children turned toward the sound, terrified

that the big man who attacked Tim would come after them. A twig snapped in the darkness a moment before a pair of yellow eyes appeared, floating like two candle flames hovering between the trees. It wasn't the man, but it was no less dangerous.

The coyote emerged slowly, its form materializing from the shadows as if the night itself brought it to life. It moved with predatory purpose, each paw descending with calculated precision as it approached the children. Its gray fur was matted, and a guttural growl vibrated from its throat, nothing like the yips they had heard when they first ran from the house. Rather, it was something malevolent. Its lips peeled back to reveal its fangs, slick with saliva that glimmered in the moonlight.

Franky grabbed Annie's hand tightly and took a slow step back. He had no knowledge of how to handle dangerous animals, but his instinct was not to make any sudden moves. Annie followed along, but tears started flowing, terrified at the carnivore menacing them.

"What do we do?" Franky asked, hoping his cousin, having grown up around there, knew more than he did.

"I don't know," she whispered. "I think we...we have to run."

The coyote took another step toward them, its growl amplified as it closed the distance on the terrified children. The animal let out a bark signaling its intent, but just as it moved to attack, a thick hand snatched it by its neck, turning the scary sounds it was making into a pained whimper. It tried to recover and turned its head to snap at the large man who grabbed it. Its teeth didn't find a home. Instead, it was met with a punch in the jaw. Clearly that was something the predator had never experienced because it seemed to throw it off, reducing the once fearsome animal to a pathetic, mewling victim. The large man raised the beast over his head and sent it crashing down, hard, to the floor.

The impact knocked the wind out of the coyote, but it wasn't beaten yet. It moved to regain its footing, but the man didn't give it a chance. He stomped on the animal's head, a sickening crunch accompanying the impact as blood erupted from its eyes, mouth, and nose. A second stomp ensured the animal would no longer pose a threat to any living creature.

There was no relief for Franky or Annie, though. Their savior was not acting out of benevolence. He just wanted the children for himself. The man's expression never changed from stone-faced wicked determination as he started toward the young ones.

"Run!" Franky shouted.

Charles had only been in the woods for a few minutes when he heard the screams. It sounded like children. That had to be Franky and his cousin. He picked up his pace as he followed the sound.

"Franky!" he shouted. "It's Dad! Follow my voice!" The woods fell silent as he continued toward the general area the sound had come from.

Charles came to a clearing and stopped, surveying

his surroundings to listen for any cues telling him where to go next. He couldn't pinpoint which way to go, and frustration snaked through him. He called to Franky again, doing his best to mask his growing anger. "Franky! Where are you?"

"Daddy!"

His son's voice came from the left, and Charles didn't hesitate to follow it, continuing to encourage the boy to use his voice. "Keep yelling!" he instructed. "It'll help me find you!"

"Daddy!" Franky said again, sounding closer. "Daddy, help!"

"Franky!"

"Daddy!"

The last shout from his son preceded the small forms materializing through the trees. Franky and Annie rushed toward their savior, with the former throwing his arms around his father as soon as he reached him, Annie following suit.

Charles didn't let the hug linger as he pulled himself from the children's grip and crouched to address them, running his hand along Franky's face to check if he was hurt. The boy recoiled instinctively at his father's touch. That pissed Charles off, and it carried in his tone despite his efforts to restrain it. "Are you okay?" he asked. "Where's the man who was after you?"

"He's back there," Annie answered when Franky didn't, like he was afraid to. "There was a coyote, and he was fighting it."

That seemed implausible, but it didn't matter. The kids were with him, and he had his gun. He would get them back to the farm and then get Susan out of there. Annie's whole family was dead, so he would leave her with the local cops. She wasn't his problem.

"Let's go," he said.

As he stood to lead the kids back to the farm, another shape emerged from the trees—a much larger one. He didn't have time to react as the big man grabbed his wrist, preventing him from using his gun. Charles wasn't physically weak, but the assailant's grip was like iron. Charles felt his wrist give way under the punishing grasp, and the revolver fell from his hand as it went numb. He clenched his left hand into a fist and swung, landing a blow on the man's jaw that did nothing. As he went to swing again, the man drove his forehead into the bridge of Charles's nose, shattering it and sending a geyser of blood gushing around the collision zone.

The impact blurred Charles's vision, and the man became an indecipherable, watery blob in the shape of a human being. Before his sight could clear, he felt the bone in his forearm snap as the man bent the arm he still held in his grip back in an unnatural angle. Charles's scream pierced the night. Satisfied, the man released him, letting him crash to the ground, his busted face splashing into the muck left behind by the rain. He tasted dirt, and his ears rang from the blow to his face, sending every sense he had into a confused tailspin, rendering him defenseless.

He tried to get back up but felt a clubbing blow on the back of his neck, sending him crashing back to the ground before he lost consciousness.

CHAPTER 20

Susan couldn't believe it when she saw Franky and Annie running toward her. When she left the house, she didn't know what direction to go, but she heard them only a moment before she saw them run past the tool shed to the rear of the house, headed toward her.

Despite the pain and weakness in her legs, she ran to embrace them, thankful they were with her and that neither the deranged killer nor her abusive husband had gotten to them first. The reprieve was short-lived, however, as she saw Wallace stalking toward them, moving with purpose, but not urgency. It was as if he had all the time in the world to catch his prey.

"Go! Get to the house!" Susan ordered the children.

She ran with them but looked back long enough to see Wallace enter the tool shed, emerging moments later with an axe.

Susan ushered the children inside and shut the

door, locking it behind her even though she knew it wouldn't hold.

"Upstairs!" she commanded. "Lock yourself in Annie's room!"

When Franky and Annie disappeared onto the second floor, she turned to the front of the house and screamed when she saw Wallace's sinister visage staring at her through the window, underlit by the jack-o'-lantern that mocked her with its grin. Too bad for the psycho, she had an equalizer in the form of the twelve-gauge shotgun she held in her hands.

Susan raised the gun and pulled the trigger. When it didn't give, her heart sank. She pumped it, ejecting a shell, and tried again, but again, it didn't fire. The damn thing must have jammed from being out in the rain.

"No!" she shouted.

Whereas the other escaped mental patients may have taken pleasure and chided her for her predicament, Wallace remained emotionless as he swung the axe into the window, shattering the glass and sending the table, along with the carved pumpkin, tumbling to the floor. The jack-o'-lantern's top popped off, and the candle rolled out.

As the large maniac stepped through the window and into the house, he tugged on the curtain, causing the rod to detach and fall to the floor, right on top of the candle. The flame ate through the thin fabric, quickly spreading across it, adding a new element of danger to the already precarious situation.

Susan needed to get to the children, but the psychopath stood between her and the stairs, brandishing his axe. She had to draw him away if she was going to get them out.

"Come on, asshole!" she yelled, before spinning on her heels and rushing into the kitchen as fast as she could. George's body still lay on the floor, but it presented an option for defense—the meat cleaver. She gripped the handle and pulled. It wasn't as easy to extricate as she would have thought, but with some effort, she got it free.

Unfortunately, the extra seconds gave Wallace the chance to catch up. She had to duck immediately to avoid the swing of the axe. The blade crashed into the cabinet above the counter. When the man pulled it free, the cabinet came with it, sending a pile of dinner plates crashing down and causing Susan to dive to her left to avoid it.

That motion brought her too close to the open cellar door. She tried to catch herself, but it was too late as she tumbled down the stairs, sending the candles flying as she crashed to the floor of the basement abattoir. Again, she wanted nothing more than to just lay there and pass out, but she saw Wallace step into view at the top of the stairs, his massive figure filling the entire door frame, the axe glinting in the light as the flames from the downed candles spread.

"Argh!" Susan cried as she crawled back toward the area where she had been held captive only a short time earlier. Panic spread as she heard Wallace descend the stairs, dragging the blade of the axe across the concrete as he reached the bottom.

She felt his presence behind her and turned,

her timing again fortuitous as she saw the axe blade hurtling toward her in an overhead arc. She rolled out of the way just in time and it sparked upon impact with the concrete. Susan stumbled to her feet and pushed past the mutilated corpses of her brother's family.

Wallace was still on her heels and swung the axe again. Susan avoided the subsequent strike as well, but it sliced into Debra's back, the corpse jolting in a rag-doll motion as the blade broke through. He was getting angry as he yanked it out, jerking the body upward in the process.

Susan landed next to Jack's body and found one final lifeline. If that didn't work, she—and the children—would not survive.

Wallace stomped toward her, the axe ready for a killing blow. Susan rolled on her back and lifted the forty-five and fired. The bullet struck the big man on the left side of his abdomen. It slowed him, but he only shrugged it off as he continued forward.

"Just fucking die!" Susan screamed as she unloaded the clip. There were nine more shots in total before the gun clicked empty. Most of them found a home in Wallace's midsection, with one hitting him directly in the throat. Each one slowed him and drove him back a little more, creating space between them. But when there were no more bullets left to fire, he was still on his feet.

Wallace was slow and unsteady, but he advanced, maintaining his grip on the axe, which had fallen to his side. He hoisted it in a two-hand grip, clearly struggling but still coming toward her.

Susan felt hopeless. She had taken her best shot—literally—and still, this man was going to kill her. She dragged herself backward but was going to run out of space in only a few more feet. Then it would be over.

Wallace pushed forward, blood gushing from all his wounds, the hole in his throat most prominently. He raised the axe one last time over his head, ready to split Susan in half. But as the weapon ascended, its weight, combined with the multiple gunshot wounds, was too much. He dropped the axe and stumbled like a drunk after last call. The man was a veritable monster, but he wasn't indestructible. He opened his mouth as if he was going to say something for the first time, but instead, blood gushed out as he released a choked gurgle and crashed to the floor. Dead.

Susan had no time to celebrate her victory. Knowing there was a fire upstairs, she pushed herself to get up and fight the pain as she made it back to the main floor.

"Franky!" she screamed as she entered the living room and saw the wall of flame blocking access to her son and niece on the second floor. She moved as close as she could and yelled again. "Franky! Annie!"

"Mommy!" Franky's voice came through the fire. "Mommy, the house is on fire!"

"I know!" Susan shouted back. "Go to Annie's room and out the window. To the roof! I'll get you down!"

"I'm scared!"

"I know, baby! But do it! Now!"

He didn't answer; she could only hope he listened. She ran outside and looked to the roof. There was an awning that wrapped around the house. She knew there was a trellis around to the right. If they could get to it, they could climb down.

Making it to a vantage point where she could see the second story, she felt anguish when she didn't see either child. And when flames erupted out of the windows on the ground floor, she felt the tears fall.

"Franky!" she screamed. "Franky, where are you?"

A moment before she lost hope entirely, she saw the right window on the second floor open. A second later, Annie stepped out and onto the roof, looking terrified. Franky followed immediately after, just as scared. Susan felt a minor surge of relief, but she had to get them down.

"To the right!" she instructed. "Climb down the trellis!"

Franky looked in the direction his mother was pointing and reached for Annie's hand. Together, the kids carefully navigated the roof toward their escape route. When they got there, they looked at each other to assess if they were really going to do this.

"What if we fall?" Annie asked.

"I'll catch you!" Susan said, not sure if she actually could. "But you have to move now!"

Annie nodded and tentatively reached over to her only way down. She hesitated for a moment before swinging herself around to the front of the structure. Once stable, she started down, making it to the ground with a little effort.

Franky followed, but when he grabbed the trellis, the slat he held onto broke, and he dangled precariously with only one hand to hold him. Susan and Annie gasped as Susan started to climb to meet him. The flames were spreading, and she could feel the intense heat blanketing the structure. Fortunately, she didn't have to, as Franky kept his balance and found a sturdier hold. Susan remained in position to climb if needed, but her son successfully made it down. As soon as all three were on the ground, Susan grabbed their hands and led them away from the inferno engulfing her brother's home.

CHAPTER 21

"Stay here," Susan told the children after getting them settled in the back of Charles's cruiser. Thankfully, the keys were inside and she was able to drive them to the edge of the property, away from the fire. "I'll be back."

"What about the bad man?" Franky asked.

"The bad men are gone," Susan replied. "All of them."

"Where are you going, Aunt Susan?" Annie asked.

"I have something to take care of," she answered. "It won't take long, I promise."

Annie nodded and hugged her cousin as Susan went around the front and found the button to pop the trunk. Thankfully, her hunch about what was back there was correct.

Susan found Charles not far into the woods behind the toolshed, lying face down. At first, she wasn't sure he was even alive. She raised the shotgun she retrieved from his vehicle. Given the way tonight had gone, she had to be ready for anything.

Initially, she went out there to find out if Charles was still alive. Yes, she brought the weapon, but it was for defense. She had already killed one man, an evil man for sure, but it didn't make her feel good. She didn't want to do it again unless she absolutely had to.

Susan approached her husband's body cautiously. She honestly didn't know if she preferred he be dead or alive. She jumped when she got the answer.

Charles gasped and coughed as he came to. He tried to raise himself up, but he could only prop himself up on one forearm, the other shattered with the bone sticking out. His face was a bloody, pulpy mess, his nose pushed to one side of his face, and he looked to be missing several teeth, but it was hard to tell for sure through the darkness and his swollen lip.

"Susan!" he gasped. "Help me!"

"Help you?" she asked.

"Yes! Damn it! I can't feel my fucking legs! I...I think he broke my back!"

Susan lowered the shotgun as she took a step. She wouldn't need it.

"Why should I help you?"

"What?" Charles said incredulously. "What the fuck are you talking about? I'm your fucking husband."

Susan held back her tears. The son of a bitch would never get another one. "You're a fucking monster is what you are," she said with more conviction than any statement she had ever made in her life.

Charles looked like he couldn't believe she was standing up to him like that. Even in this vulnerable state, he still thought he could control her. "So I was a little rough on you," he said. "It was only for your own good. This world is a tough place. I made you tougher."

"Tougher?" Susan asked through gritted teeth.

"Yeah!" he said, the mask slipping as he understood he wasn't holding the cards. "Look at you! Last I saw you, you were tied up in the basement! Now, look at you! You're out! You're tough, baby!"

Susan laughed and shook her head. "You're pathetic," she told her husband. "You were so angry and bitter at your failures that you took it out on your wife and son. Because of you, we live in constant fear— fear of a man who's supposed to love and care for us. Well, no more."

"You don't have to be afraid of me, Susan! Please! I...I love you!"

"And I loved you. But you aren't that person anymore. You're no different than those men who tried to kill us."

Charles twisted from panic back to anger. Even at that moment he couldn't control it. "So, what? You're going to kill me?"

For a moment, she had forgotten she was holding the shotgun. She looked at it before turning back to Charles. "No," she said defiantly.

As the word left her mouth, she heard motion from behind Charles. There was something out there. Multiple somethings.

"So, what?" Charles blurted. "What the fuck are you going to do?"

Susan saw a pair of yellow eyes pierce through the darkness directly behind her wounded abuser. Soon, another joined it. Then another. Predators ready to devour one of their own. "Nothing," she said. "Goodbye, Charles."

Charles was too stunned to respond.

Susan turned and walked back toward the farm, not looking back as her husband screamed under the jaws of the coyotes.

Susan deposited the shotgun back into the trunk and pushed it closed. The fire had completely spread, and the roof had buckled into itself, the amber flames erupting from within.

The weary woman walked around and sat in the driver's seat, taking a moment to look at the children in the backseat. They were both asleep, Annie's head nestled against Franky's shoulder. Susan felt unimaginable sadness looking at her niece, knowing her entire family had been killed. Though she was numb at the moment, the grieving would come, and she would have to figure out the logistics of caring for Annie. But first, they needed to get to the police.

Susan started the car and drove away from the burning home. As she pulled to the edge of the driveway, ready to turn onto the road, she caught a glimpse of the quartz clock in the vehicle's dashboard. It said it was six minutes past twelve. Mischief Night was over.

Happy Halloween.

EPILOGUE

1998

It was early spring in Atlantic City, New Jersey. While the boardwalk wasn't as bustling as it would be during the summer months, the weather was nice enough that a good number of people were out and about.

The man in the black suit sat on a bench outside one of the many casinos that lined the strip. The glitzy monuments lured folks in with the promise of the chance to make all their dreams come true. But when that promise inevitably went unrealized, they would spit those dreamers out with little more than the shirts on their back.

The man savored a lick of his soft-serve vanilla ice cream cone. It was hot where he came from, so any chance he had to cool down was a welcome one. As the sweet, sugary cream soothed his throat, the man watched as one of the aforementioned unlucky dreamers stumbled out of the casino onto the boardwalk.

He wore a suit not all that dissimilar to the man on the bench, but it was completely disheveled, with one flap of his white dress shirt untucked and hanging below his belt. His collar was undone, and his tie was loosened. A tan blotch to the left of it betrayed that he had spilled his coffee.

A truly pathetic-looking specimen, the man reached into his jacket pocket and retrieved a soft pack of Marlboros. He bounced it in his hand a couple times. When no cigarette popped out, he stuck his finger in the opening and rooted around like he was performing a prostate exam. When he finally accepted that the pack was empty, he crushed it in his hands and spiked it on the ground, punctuating the act with a flurry of expletives.

Hmm, the man on the bench thought as he observed the gambler rapidly cycling through his emotions. *Perhaps I should offer this poor soul some assistance.* Before he could act, however, a shadow fell over him. He looked up to see the person he had been waiting for.

The guy was painfully average in almost every way. Average height. Average build. Medium-length hair and a five-o'clock shadow. There was nothing special about him at all. At least not yet. The only thing that stood out about him was the leather motorcycle jacket he wore. The man on the bench couldn't see the back of it from his current vantage point, but he knew what was on it—a bloody, grinning skull patch and the words Hell's Horde, M.C.

Normally a biker like him would appear intimidating, but the man on the bench wasn't one to cower before anyone. Besides, this one had an expression that could only be described as giddy.

"How the hell did you do it, man?" the biker asked.

The man smiled and took another lick of ice cream before addressing him. "How are you, Caleb? Judging by your expression, I'd venture to guess you're well?"

"Well?" Caleb asked, as if that was the understatement of the century. He sat on the bench next to the man without waiting for an invitation. It didn't bother the man. An amused smile pursed his lips as Caleb continued his inquiry. "For real, man, what did you do?"

"I don't follow."

"Bro, don't bullshit me. You come into the bar while I'm all in my cups, tell me I should talk to Vicki even though she's never even looked my way, and I end up taking her home?" Caleb spewed the lengthy question without taking a breath. Like the man observed—he was giddy.

"You just needed a little pep talk, Caleb. You should give yourself more credit," the man said, taking a bite of the waffle cone, enjoying the medley of its crisp mixed with the cool ice cream.

"Uh huh," Caleb replied skeptically. He pulled out a small black card with a phone number etched in gold lettering. "So, what's this, then?"

"A business card," the man replied. Normally this coy routine would annoy even the most congenial person, but the biker was so stupid happy about that girl the man could mash what was left of his cone on his head and he would probably laugh it off.

Even so, Caleb adopted a more business-like tone. "You left this on my bike. I ain't stupid, man. I know you did something that helped me with Vicki, and I appreciate it even if I don't understand it." He paused, getting legitimately serious for the first time. "Now, I imagine you want something from me? So, what is it?"

"You're a very skeptical man, Caleb."

Caleb laughed as he retrieved a pack of Marlboro Lights from his pocket. He popped a cigarette in his mouth, cupping his hands around the tip to shield the flame as he lit it. "Yeah, well, you don't run in my circles without developing a healthy amount of distrust toward your fellow man."

He went to return the pack to the inside pocket of his vest, but the man held his hand out. "Mind if I bum a smoke?"

"Sure," Caleb said, plucking a cigarette out and handing it over.

The man accepted it and rolled it in his hand, studying it curiously.

"Light?" Caleb asked, holding out his Zippo.

"Saving it for later," the man said, depositing the cigarette behind his ear as Caleb put the lighter back in his pocket.

The men sat in silence for a minute. Caleb smoked his cigarette while the man ate his ice cream cone.

When the man was finished, it was he that spoke first. "You're a smart, capable man, Caleb. If this Vicki girl has developed an affection for you, that has much more to do with what you bring to the table than anything I could offer."

The biker blushed. A grown man aligned with a crew of badasses was actually blushing because a girl liked him.

The man continued. "And it's because of what you bring the table that I want to offer you a job."

Caleb perked up. "What kind of job?" He eyed the man's suit. "I ain't exactly the nine-to-five type."

The man laughed. "I don't need an accountant, Caleb. I need a man of your talents. Your talents and, let's say, *moral flexibility*."

"What's that mean?"

The man stood and tossed his balled up napkin into the nearby trashcan. He stepped in front of Caleb and buttoned his suit jacket. "Tomorrow night. Lola's Diner. You know the spot?"

"Sure."

"Meet me there at nine p.m. I'll give you the details then. It has the potential to be very lucrative for you... and your motorcycle club."

Caleb cocked a brow. "Good for the club?"

"Yes, Caleb," the man said with a smile. "I imagine you being responsible for a large influx of cash will go a long way toward your standing with your compatriots?"

"Green is a universal fucking language," Caleb agreed.

"Excellent. See you tomorrow at Lola's. Nine p.m. sharp."

Caleb nodded, and the man turned and walked off down the boardwalk. He enjoyed the breeze as he strolled, watching the diverse menagerie of the human animal going about its business.

The guy in the disheveled suit leaned forward on the rail separating the boardwalk from the beach, looking forlorn, his head in his hands.

The man grinned widely as he pulled the cigarette from behind his ear and approached the degenerate gambler resting against the railing. The sad sack felt the man's presence and looked at him with bloodshot eyes hovering over tear-stained cheeks.

"Smoke?" the man asked, holding out the cigarette between his thumb and forefinger.

The desperate man only hesitated slightly before accepting it. "Thanks," he muttered sheepishly as he patted his pockets, looking for a lighter.

"Here," the man said, holding up the Zippo that had been in Caleb's pocket right before he left. "Let me get that." The man snapped the lighter open and flicked the flint wheel. The flame was strong even with the wind blowing off the Atlantic Ocean. When the cigarette was lit, he snapped it shut and returned it to his pocket.

The gambler turned back to look over the water as he took the first coveted drag off the cigarette. The man could tell he was ashamed to look him in the eye.

"Rough night?" the man asked.

The gambler blew a plume of smoke out of his nostrils and answered while still avoiding eye contact. "You could say that."

"How bad?"

"Pretty fucking bad," the gambler said as he turned to the man. "What's it to you?"

The man shrugged. "Truthfully, it's nothing to me." He reached into his jacket and pulled out a black poker chip, holding it out to the man the same way he did the cigarette. "But it could be everything to you."

The gambler hesitated, but the man thrust his hand farther, encouraging the guy to take the chip. After a long moment of contemplation, he accepted it. "Th-thanks," he said, again looking down.

"Now, listen to me carefully, Marty," the man started.

"How do you know—"

The man didn't let him finish the question. "You're wasting time, Marty. Focus."

Marty nodded and shut his mouth as the man continued, pointing to the entryway of the casino behind him. "Take this chip and go inside to the third roulette table on the left once you get off the escalator. When you see four, then twenty-three, come out, place this on double zero for the next spin. At thirty-eight to one, you'll walk away with $3,800. Will that be enough to look your wife in the eye when you get home?"

"Yeah, but how do you know?"

The man smirked. "Maybe I don't, but what do you have to lose?"

"Nothing, I guess."

"Exactly," the man said, reaching into his jacket one more time and producing a black business card with a phone number etched in gold lettering. He held it out to Marty, who accepted it.

"What's this?" Marty asked, perplexed.

"If I'm right and you hit that bet, all I'm asking in

return is a conversation. So cash out your winnings, go home, and take Ellen to a nice dinner."

"How do—"

The man cut him off again. "Enjoy your weekend, then call me on Monday. I may have a very lucrative opportunity for you. But go now. Clock's ticking." The man shooed Marty away.

The confused gambler stamped out the cigarette and started toward the casino. After a few steps, he stopped and turned back to the man, who was still leaning against the rail, watching Marty like a proud father sending his kid to college. "Who are you?" Marty asked.

Ba'al's grin stretched wide across his face.

"Call me Bill."

If you, or someone you know has been the victim of domestic violence, help is available throught the National Domestic Violence Hotline.

1-800-799-SAFE (7233)
OR
Text *Start* to 88788
www.thehotline.org

AFTERWORD

Thank you so much for reading *Mischief Night!*

This was a fun novella to write. My earliest experiences with horror movies were in the 1980s, so Slashers were a big part of my initiation into the genre. Unkillable masked pyschopaths that systematically eliminate groups of horny teens one-by-one until they are taken out by the final girl? Sign me up!

While this isn't my first rodeo when it comes to writing a slasher story, it is my attempt to pay homage to one of the first movies in the genre I ever saw. One that was, is, and will always be my favorite. Can you guess which one it is? I'm talking, of course, about John Carpenter's seminal classic, *Halloween.*

This book originally started as a piece of Halloween fan fiction. I always thought it would be a fun idea to see what happened to the other inmates Michael Myers broke out as a diversion when he escaped in 1978. With that in mind, I set out writing a story just like that, taking place in the Halloween universe. It was just for fun. I was releasing an unedited chapter each month for my free VIP Readers Club (shameless side note - you can find out more about my VIP Readers Club in the next section). It was fun playing around in the sandbox of the world of my favorite horror movie, but, halfway through writing it, I decided I like the story enough to publish it! Of course, I couldn't use characters and locations from the movie, so I went back through and reworked it into the story you just finished (unless you skipped right to the afterword, but who does that?).

I wasn't trying to reinvent the wheel here. My goal was to tell a solid, classic slasher story with a few twists and turns that hopefully didn't play out like you expect (like Jack getting unceremoniously blown away in Chapter 17) and kept you entertained throughout.

I also hope the epilogue left you wanting a little more. If you're curious about Caleb and Bill, you can see what happens next in my book, Pursuit, available now wherever books are sold! If you think Jack and his cronies were nasty pieces of work, wait until you meet The Rider.

Before I let you go, I want to ask a small favor. If you enjoyed this book, please consider leaving a review. I can't emphasize enough how much reader reviews help independent publishers like Horror House Publishing get their books in the hands of readers who may not have discovered us otherwise. So, if you can spare a few minutes, I'd really appreciate it!

Review Mischief Night on Amazon

Review Mischief Night on Goodreads

Thank you so much for your support!

June 9, 2025

ABOUT THE AUTHOR

James Kaine is a bestselling author, publisher and filmmaker born and raised in Trenton, NJ. An active pro member of the Horror Writer's Association, he brings readers visceral, haunting tales of terror via his *Horror House Publishing* imprint.

BookLife by Publisher's Weekly proclaimed his novel, *The Dead Children's Playground*, "will chill readers to the bone." The book, the first in his *American Horrors* anthology series, has been a #1 bestseller in U.S. Horror on Amazon, a reader selection for the 2025 Books of Horror Indie Brawl and is being translated into multiple languages, bringing James's cinematic style of scary storytelling to a global audience.

He resides in Hamilton, NJ with his wife, Jessica, their two children and an energetic Boston Terrier. When he isn't writing he loves to read, travel, cook, watch movies and learn new skills.

Become a Kaineiac and get exclusive stories, first-look news and discounts by joining James's free VIP Reader club at **www.jameskaine.com**.

For bookings, media inquiries and any other requests, send an email to **james@jameskaine.com**.

BECOME A KAINEIAC!

Sign up for the James Kaine VIP Readers Club and get these great benefits:

- A free eBook just for signing up!

- Bonus content!

- New release alerts!

- First news - new projects, cover reveals, upcoming appearances and more!

- Monthly merch discounts for my web store!

- Indie author spotlights!

- Contests and giveaways!

There is never any cost be a member and you can unsubscribe at any time and keep your free book on me! Scan the code below or visit **www.jameskaine.com** to sign up!

BOOKS BY JAMES KAINE

MY PET WEREWOLF SERIES

My Pet Werewolf

Gunther

AMERICAN HORRORS SERIES

The Dead Children's Playground

Devil of the Pines

STANDALONE

Pursuit

Black Friday

Mischief Night